CRACKER

TRUE ROMANCE

CRACKER

TRUE ROMANCE

Liz Holliday

Virgin

First published in Great Britain in 1996 by
Virgin Books
an imprint of Virgin Publishing Ltd
332 Ladbroke Grove
London W10 5AH

Cracker © Granada Television and Jimmy McGovern

Text copyright © Liz Holliday 1996
from a screenplay by Paul Abbott

Cover photographs © Granada Television, 1995

ISBN 0 7535 0035 3

Typeset by Galleon Typesetting, Ipswich
Printed and bound in Great Britain by
Mackays of Chatham PLC

Acknowledgements

Special thanks to Peter Darvill Evans, my editor at
Virgin Publishers, for his extreme patience; to Andy Lane for
listening to me whinge; and to Peter Garratt for his advice.
Thanks also, as ever, to Alex Stewart, Barbara Morris,
Martin Weaver, 3SF, and everyone from The Roadtrip.

For Karen, wherever she may be

ONE

'Two,' Fitz said, peering at his client over the rim of his spectacles. He hoped he didn't sound as bored, or as hung-over, as he felt.

It was an old exercise, one he used routinely on the worst of the whiners and the whingers, the people who could have sorted out their own problems if they'd only tried a bit harder. The point of the exercise was to get her to think for herself, instead of letting Fitz fill her head with ideas.

'He's never forgotten my birthday,' the woman conceded after a long moment's thought.

'Three,' Fitz said. The trick was not to let her stop to think – to let her surprise herself finding out what her subconscious really thought.

She was the wrong side of forty, dressed in a pale suit that probably hadn't cost as much as she wished, but which set off her dark auburn hair to perfection. Toner on that hair, Fitz thought: she'd probably forgotten what her own colour was underneath it; and she wouldn't want reminding that the answer was probably salt and pepper shading to grey. She wasn't pretty, but she'd learnt to use cosmetics to make the most of what she had.

'If he's late home he can usually come up with a good

excuse,' she said. She perched on the edge of a hard chair. Fitz had offered her one of the armchairs that cluttered his office, but she'd turned him down. 'I'm not always convinced,' she added, almost without pause. 'Does that count?'

'Four,' Fitz said, not bothering to tell her it counted if she thought it did. They'd already been through that with points one and two.

'He doesn't smoke,' she said.

'Five,' Fitz said quickly, glad she was getting through the points. She'd turned up unexpectedly, and his receptionist had fitted her into a late cancellation. Fitz had been looking forward to an early afternoon off – a *skint* early afternoon off. He'd agreed to see her intending to limit the session to some exploratory discussion to see where her problems lay – that was the usual format in a first session. But the woman had come in, announced herself as Rene, plonked herself on the chair and launched into a diatribe about her husband's shortcomings. Before Fitz had even discovered her surname he found himself counselling her.

It was the same old rubbish, anyway – low-level irritations leading to high-level rows, the whole thing fuelled by the realisation that their lives were slipping away, moment by moment, each blaming the other for days not lived to the full, paths not taken and other choices not explored.

Fitz was bored with it, bored with listening to the same problems clothed in different words, day after endless bloody day. They none of them had the insight to see what to do to save themselves or the guts to do anything about it if they did.

2

'I haven't finished,' Rene said determinedly. 'He doesn't smoke unless we've had a row. Then he lights up in the greenhouse.'

Fitz tried again. 'We'll call that five for being considerate?' He was suddenly conscious of the cigarette dangling from his fingers and the blue smoke wreathing up from it. Sod it, he thought, and took a long drag. It was his office, after all.

'He's stunted my tomatoes,' the woman said. 'Eighteen months, fifteen plants – nothing.' Twenty-five years, Fitz thought. That came to nothing, too. 'We'll call it four for being a shite,' Rene concluded.

Fitz suppressed a sigh. He swivelled round on his chair, feeling the inertia of his great bulk holding him back. 'Come on, Rene. Twenty good points to finish the exercise.' Get it over with, let me go home, he thought. They'd started with twenty bad points – she'd had no problem with those. It was supposed to let her vent her feelings harmlessly: then the exercise moved on to the good things so she'd leave on a positive note. Only she'd got stuck like a car going round and round Spaghetti Junction, endlessly revisiting the same stretches of road – her husband's lack of consideration, in this case.

'No,' Rene said flatly. 'He's had four more than he deserves.' She opened the flap of her handbag and fumbled for her purse. 'You're right, you know – I'm wasted on him.'

Fitz jerked his head up. '*I'm* right?' he demanded. It was the last thing he wanted – clients pushing the responsibility for the decisions they made on to him.

Her eyes widened in anger, and in that moment Fitz could see all the years of anger and pain, all the bitter arguments written on her face. 'Twenty-five years I've wasted on him,' she said. She had her purse out now, and began to undo it. Her movements were fast and jerky, as if they were physical expressions of her inner fury. 'And what do I end up with? Sitting in a clinic with a bloody – no offence meant – a bloody shrink with a hangover.' She had the money out, and she stared at it for a second as she muttered. 'I'm better than this.' She stood up and crossed the room. 'Thanks very much, Doctor Fitzgerald,' she said, thrusting a wad of notes in his face. 'You've opened my mind. You have.' Fitz took the cash. 'You're a very clever man – I'll never forget it.' She turned and hurried out of the room.

Not clever enough, Fitz thought gloomily as he stared at the money. 'Most patients tend to need more than just the one session,' he said. Clever enough would have spun things out for a couple of months at least.

Rene turned as she got to the door. 'Oh no,' she said. Her smile was hard and tight. 'Best fifty I've ever spent.' She hurried out, clutching her bag – Fitz noted that, noted the way she held it to her like a baby, like a comfort blanket, and decided she was nowhere near as happy with her decision as she thought she was. Not that he'd ever persuade her of it. The door slammed behind her.

Fitz counted the notes she'd given him. Fifty pounds in used fivers. At least it was cash – the bank manager need never know he'd had it.

'Bye,' Fitz said to the closed door.

It was like something out of a fairytale, Janice thought. Cinderella arriving at the ball in a dress made of fairy

4

lace and satin couldn't have looked more beautiful than Nina did, stepping out of the bridal car as if it were a coach made from a pumpkin touched by dream-dust and magic.

Lucky Nina, Janice thought. Nina has it all. It was the way it should be, of course. Nina was beautiful and kind, and when she came up the stairs to the church on their father's arm, Janice couldn't resent it – couldn't resent everything Nina already had, everything she was going to have in the future.

Janice had her dreams, but she kept them locked up tight in her heart where no one could see them, no one could laugh at them, no one could tell her she was being silly.

So she stood on the church steps, just one of the cluster of bridesmaids, as pretty in their floral dresses as the posies they clutched, and as Nina came up those stairs with their father, Janice couldn't look away. She felt as if she would burst with love and pride – love and pride enough to keep those secret thoughts, those deeper secrets, down in the dark place of the heart where they belonged.

'How are you feeling?' she asked, as soon as Nina came close enough. She touched her sister on the arm, while their other sister, Louise, looked on from the cluster of bridesmaids.

'Bit nervous,' Nina admitted. She smoothed the yards of veil that swept back from her golden hair and set off her high cheekbones and perfect violet eyes.

Behind her, their father smiled at them.

'You'll be fine, you know,' Janice said. 'Oh, it'll go like a whistle.'

Their father, smiling at them – at all his pretty daughters, that's what he would say – moved closer.

Closer to Nina, anyway – Nina who had everything.

'Nina,' Janice said. 'You look so beautiful . . .' It was more than she could stand – Nina in that dress, with all eyes on her and a man who loved her waiting for her inside the church, and all these people standing here who loved her – it made Janice want to weep, for all the things her sister had. All the things she, Janice, could never have. She threw herself at Nina. The crisp net of the veil crumpled in her hands, and the smell of Nina's perfume – all rose and musk – and her hairspray made Janice's head swim. 'It makes me want to cry,' she said.

'Don't,' Louise said from behind her. '*Don't* cry.'

Nina pulled away. 'I'm fine, Janice,' she said, her voice full of familiar impatience.

And she was – there were no tears in her eyes, nothing to smear that perfect make-up, or redden those milk-white cheeks. It was always the same: they never understood how she felt, that she felt too much and couldn't hold it in, could never hold it in to achieve the perfection they managed without thought. No, she wasn't like them, and they'd never forgiven her for it.

Their father came between them. 'You ready, love?' he asked. He moved in close, and touched the small of Nina's back with one protective hand. Then he kissed her gently on the cheek. 'I'm so proud of you,' he said. He turned to Louise, including her in that statement. She patted the front of his waistcoat, smoothing down imaginary wrinkles. He smiled at her, at his other pretty daughter. Then he came round to Nina's other side. His gaze drifted over Janice, but he barely seemed to see her.

6

The Wedding March struck up from within the church. He led his daughter in, and Janice could only follow.

It was a fine day. Judith Fitzgerald was walking her new baby in the park, and for once her husband was with her. She should have been gloriously happy.

She wasn't. She was steaming. She'd made sure Fitz knew it, too. He trailed along behind her. She knew he was busy thinking up excuses, but she didn't care. She was so used to dealing with them that she could have done it in her sleep. Or at least, could have if it wouldn't have set him off on another one of his bloody psychoanalytical tirades.

He just couldn't see that their problems were simple: money and sex. The amount he spent over the amount he earned, and the fact that he was still puppydogging around over that damned stick insect of a bit on the side of his.

Stick insect. Judith had started calling her that while she was pregnant with baby James – about the same time she'd taken to wearing her shirts outside her trousers, in fact. Judith was still wearing her shirts outside her trousers. She still thought of Jane Penhaligon as a stick insect.

But Jane Penhaligon wasn't the issue at hand right now. The issue at hand was money. Or the lack of it, to be more precise.

'Eighty,' Fitz said. He'd had to think about it. 'I gave you eighty last Friday.'

'Sixty and it was Wednesday,' Judith countered. In the pram, James smiled at the world. Windy, like your father, Judith thought at him, refusing to be cheered. A vagrant breeze brought the smell of Fitz's cigarette smoke to her. She scowled at James. At least Fitz had promised not to smoke around the baby.

'I paid for the groceries, Saturday,' Fitz said, in a voice loud enough so the whole park could hear. A woman helping a child up the slide in the swings gave her a wry smile as they went by.

'Ten pounds cigarettes, twenty-two pounds booze, sixteen pounds food,' Judith snapped. 'You paid by Switch and put it on the overdraft.' Case proven, M'lud, she thought. This man is congenitally incapable of maintaining family life and shouldn't be allowed. She could almost feel Fitz opening his mouth to make a comeback. 'The bank wants the cards destroyed,' she said, before he could do so.

Silence. Blessed peace for a moment or two. She realised she couldn't hear Fitz's feet scrunching on the gravel behind her.

'Done!' he said from a good way behind her.

She turned. He was standing by a litter bin and holding up the Switch card – the credit cards had long since been cut up – and as soon as he was sure he had her attention, he dropped it into the bin.

Judith flicked the brake lever down on the pram. Then she stalked over to Fitz. She leaned right over to fish the card out of the bottom of the bin, telling herself it was definitely time to start her step classes again. Or at least yoga.

Got it! she thought triumphantly. She waved it in Fitz's face, hoping she didn't look as red as she felt. 'You are worth more to me dead than alive right now,

Fitz.' She glared at him. 'Do not joke.'

She turned and went back to the pram, leaving Fitz behind her. For once he was speechless.

Nina danced with her father while the music played and all the guests watched. His hand was on the small of her back, his cheek an inch or two from hers. He smelled of whisky and aftershave, and it made her think of so many things, of summer afternoons and being a child, of winter nights and trying to sleep, waiting to sleep snuggled up under the blankets, of praying for sleep to come.

But she wasn't a child now, and Colin was watching – Colin who was her husband now, had been for a whole hour and a half. Her Colin, now that she was a woman and not a child.

And Janice, of course, watching it all: Janice who didn't understand, but who was jealous anyway – Janice watching from the side, with tears in her eyes.

Fitz had fifty pounds in his pocket – fifty pounds for wrecking a marriage, or for saving a woman's life, depending how you looked at it.

He'd planned to give it to Judith when he met her in the park, until she'd started in on him about money before he'd even had time to open his mouth.

So he'd kept the cash and threatened to throw the card away. Well, he'd thought it was funny at the time.

In retrospect, maybe not.

Either way, he still had fifty quid in his pocket. On the way home from the park, he made his excuses and left. The bookie's wasn't far away.

The air inside was blue with cigarette smoke and thick with tension. Overhead, TV screens flickered. A race was just ending. The commentator's voice rose to a scream as the horses pelted towards the finish. London Pride, for sure, Fitz thought in the split second he had left – it was a certainty, a nose ahead of the field; and then some other bugger came nosing up on the inside and won by a short neck.

Hell with that then, Fitz thought. He'd planned to take it easy – have a few little ten-quid bets, make the money last. Instead he plonked the lot down on Mary Dear in the four-thirty at Newmarket – last race of the day.

Anything to avoid going home.

Colin was drunk. Very, very drunk. So drunk that Dave Marshall had to get him to the bogs in a hurry.

'Wouldn't want to barf down your lovely wife's lovely dress, would you?' he said, waving a bottle of some posh German beer under Colin's nose.

'No mate,' Colin agreed. He'd have agreed to anything, happy as he was. It'd taken him so long to get Nina to agree to marry him that he couldn't bear the thought of anything going wrong. When he'd asked the first time and she'd said no, he'd felt humiliated. Then raging with anger. But it wasn't as if she'd wanted to break things off, and when she'd finally said yes it was like he'd earned it – earned her, by being patient and waiting till she was ready. After all, she was so innocent for all she was twenty-seven.

And now she was his, all his, he thought as he stumbled out of the toilet, followed by Dave who stumbled and had to make a grab for the door jamb to stay upright.

'Colin!' a voice said from beside him.

He looked round. Nina's sister Janice was standing by the door. She was all right, was Janice – pretty enough in her way, though not a patch on his Nina. And too clever by half, that was what Colin thought. No wonder she couldn't get herself a fella, always talking about her job at the college.

He grinned at her. 'Hey Janice!' he called. He went over to her, walking carefully to be sure his feet landed where he expected them to.

'There's some big lads in there, Janice,' Dave said. 'You're missing out.'

'Piss off,' Janice snarled. That was her all over, Colin thought – reckoned she was too good by half, too good for a bit of a laugh, at any rate.

Dave grinned and waved bye-bye at her, and started to go back into the party with the others. Colin made to follow him, but Janice got in his way. She looked upset.

She was Nina's sister after all, Colin thought. Wasn't her fault if she didn't even know how to get herself a dance at a wedding do. 'Take no notice, Janice,' he said. He pulled out a packet of cigarettes and shoved one in his mouth. 'Here, have you met Jimmy Cowgill? Best of the bunch –' He wasn't a bad bloke, Jimmy. Done well for himself. Him and Janice would make a good pair. Good couple, even – that'd get Janice out of Nina's hair. Colin grabbed Janice's arm and pulled her over in the direction of the window, where Jimmy and a couple of other blokes were discussing the football. 'Cowie!' he shouted.

Jimmy looked round, but before Colin could call him over Janice pulled free. 'I want to talk to you!' she said.

'Over here!' Colin called.

'I want to talk to you,' Janice hissed. She stared at him – that stare she seemed to wear whenever Nina was around – and Colin suddenly remembered why he'd thought she was a bit odd in the first place.

Janice knew what she had to do. You couldn't hope for a happy ending unless you were strong and brave and honest. So she got Colin to come outside with her, to the back of the hall where the big industrial rubbish bins fought for space with the car park where an old man was slowly washing his car. There was a faint smell of old booze and rotting rubbish, but that was all right. Just as long as he would listen to her.

She made sure she had his full attention, and then she told him what she knew. All of it.

'I don't believe that,' he said. He'd walked off before she finished, leaving her standing on the top of the few shallow steps that led up to the hall. Now he stood staring at the rubbish bins. He wouldn't look at her.

'You have to,' Janice said. She had right on her side, after all. 'It's true!'

He whirled round and came marching back to her. 'You're a liar,' he said.

If he didn't believe her after all – after the risk she'd taken . . . She couldn't bear it. 'I'm not,' she said. She hated the way her voice sounded – like a whiney little schoolgirl's.

Colin came up the steps. 'What are you playing at?' he demanded. He had a half-empty bottle of beer in his

12

hand. 'This is like . . . this is today, for Christ's sake.'
He waved the bottle in her face. 'What are you playing
at? Do you know what you just said?'

'I thought you'd want to know.' Janice was shaken.
Surely he'd want to know, rather than having to guess?
He was so strong, so good-looking. She had been sure
he could stand to know the truth.

'Why the hell would I want to know *that*, Janice?' He
was glaring at her now – reminding her of someone, but
she couldn't quite place the face. 'Why would you want
to tell me that? On my bloody wedding day!'

Janice took a deep breath. She could feel the tears
starting to come, but she wasn't going to cry. That had
been the number one rule, ever since she was a child.
Never let them see you cry. Never let him see you cry.

To be a fairytale princess, you have to be strong, but
you have to be true as well. 'Because I like you,' she
whispered in the face of his anger. It was true. Nina
loved him. How could Janice do any less?

But it didn't help. Colin turned and hurled his bottle
of beer across the yard. It crashed into the wall and
booze splattered everywhere. The old man started to say
something, then stopped.

Janice stared at Colin. His chest was heaving under
his morning suit. He started into the hall. Then he came
back down.

He stood very close to her. She could smell his
aftershave under the alcohol. 'You want your frigging
head seeing to, you do,' he said into her ear.

Then he left.

She stood there for a while longer, determined not to
cry, even though there was no one to see her. He's a boy,

she thought to herself fiercely. That's all he is — a know-nothing little boy.

Nina knew how to please a man. She knew the things to do. She stood in front of Colin and she slowly unbuttoned his shirt. That was good. You went slowly — wound them up, button by button, kept them waiting until they couldn't wait any longer.

Colin's skin was smooth under his shirt. She put her hand flat against his chest, momentarily entranced by the novelty of that smoothness, of the skin taut over flat slabs of muscle. She moved her hand down, almost unwillingly, to his fly — to reveal that secret place, the place you weren't supposed to think about, to talk about. But she knew — she'd seen, she'd talked about it late at night to Louise.

She knew how to please a man, Nina did.

But then Colin's hand covered her own. For a moment she thought he was urging her on. But he stopped her, pulled her hand away. Denied her the right to please him. She looked up at him, appalled.

'I can't,' he said. He must have seen the hurt in her eyes. 'I've had too much to drink.'

It was a lie. His eyes said it. So did the hardness beneath her hand.

So he was teasing her, that was all — the way men liked to tease, to pretend that it was all your idea when really they wanted it all so badly, and the only way you could stop them wanting was to give them everything.

Nina knew that game. She felt safe with that game. 'No you haven't,' she said, looking down coyly at his crotch.

He didn't say anything, so she started to slide her fingers beneath his shirt again, feeling the warm silkiness of his skin beneath her hands, knowing she could please him. She leaned forward to kiss him. She was tall but he was taller, and when he moved away she couldn't reach.

'Can't we just leave it?' he pleaded, and she suddenly realised he wasn't teasing. He didn't want her. Didn't want the thing she'd been prepared to give him – had *wanted* to give him. It was all she could offer, and he was rejecting it.

'For God's sake, Colin,' she said. 'It's our wedding night.'

'I'm just drunk,' he said. He started pulling his shirt back round him, like she repelled him. Like she was a bad girl, or something.

'Right,' she said. She pushed past him into the bathroom and locked the door.

She leaned against the sink unit so she didn't have to look at her face in the mirror, but she wouldn't cry. Good girls don't cry.

Janice was just a little bit drunk when she got back to her flat. She was carrying Nina's bouquet, which she'd caught to a volley of cheers and whistles.

Before she took her coat off she found a vase for it – such a cheap vase, she thought, for such beautiful flowers. She filled it with water and put the bouquet in it, then set the whole thing down on the table.

She'd caught the bouquet. If you listened to them, that meant she was going to be the next one to get married. Well perhaps she might. But not if it meant wedding a stupid boy like Colin.

Janice knew what she wanted, and it didn't include marrying a stupid cocky *boy*.

Nina stared at herself in the mirror. She was going to have to face him soon, unless she wanted to spend the whole night in the bathroom. She smoothed her hair back, took a deep breath and went out.

Colin was sitting on the edge of the bed, staring at the floor between his feet. Nina went and stood in front of him, but she found that she couldn't say anything.

He looked up at her. 'I'm sorry,' he said. 'It isn't that I don't want you, you know that.'

'You aren't drunk, though, are you Colin?'

'No,' he said. 'It was . . .' He started again. 'At the reception. Janice. She said –'

A chill went through Nina. 'Oh, so that's it,' she cut in. 'She spun you some tale about what Dad's supposed to have done to me, didn't she?'

He nodded.

'Well, let me tell you something,' Nina said. Tell him what, though? What she told everyone else. 'It's a pack of lies. Attention seeking, that's all it is. That and jealousy.' He stared up at her. He has to believe me, Nina thought. Otherwise I've got nothing. Like Janice. Nothing. 'She just can't bear the fact that I've got you and she's never managed to keep a boyfriend.' She was surprised at the rage in her voice. By the look on his face, so was Colin.

'So it's not true, then?' His eyes were dark in the lamplight, almost black.

Nina took a deep breath. 'No,' she said. She reached

16

out and touched his hand. His fingers curled round hers, and they stood for a moment like that. Then he stood up and pulled her to him.

It isn't true if I don't want it to be, she thought. If I never think about it again, maybe it never happened. And she kissed him.

TWO

Janice was almost too excited to concentrate on what she was doing, which was fixing a biofeedback monitor dropped by some no-brain student.

Sunday had been bad. Sunday had been very bad, in fact, with nothing to think about but Nina and Colin off on their honeymoon, and the look of contempt in Colin's eyes when he said she – she could remember his exact words, the precise inflection of his voice, and the mingled scents of aftershave and alcohol – should have her brain examined. Her frigging brain.

Well, that had been Saturday. This was Monday, and today there was a lecture by Doctor Edward Fitzgerald – Fitz to those who knew him well – which was why Janice was excited. Her hands started to shake, just enough so her soldering iron touched the wrong connection. She swore under her breath as the circuit desoldered itself.

Correcting her mistake took all her concentration, and just as she'd finished voices from outside the door broke the silence. The door opened and a group of students came in, arguing. Janice knew them – Carol, the head of the Student Union Entertainments Committee, and Frank and John, a couple of her cronies.

None of them paid any attention to Janice.

19

'– not paying two hundred quid for a crap band,' John said. 'And anyway you should –'

Carol darted past John. Janice saw she was carrying an electrical resistance unit. 'Are you saying we should book *your* band?' She put the machine on the work-surface and turned back to the two lads.

'We could do a lot worse,' Frank said. He was on the short side, and slightly built, with a frizz of hair that might have suited him better shorter, and a face that would only ever be interesting and not handsome. He smiled at Carol, but she ignored him and went over to John.

She was standing close to him – so close to him, when she already had a boyfriend of her own. Janice knew what she was like – like Nina and Louise. She knew how to play the game. How to please them, how to tease them.

'You do that for charity?' Carol asked, staring up into John's eyes. 'For free?'

John laughed. 'Course not –' He was well built, with eyes that knew how to smile and a slightly lopsided smile that lent interest to a face that would otherwise have been far too good-looking to be interesting. Of course he wasn't giving anything away for free. What man ever did?

But oh, if he would just look at her like that . . . if she could just be a bit more like them, a bit less like herself in her frumpy white lab coat and sensible flat shoes.

'Is that the Union Ball?' Janice asked. Maybe it wasn't too late. Maybe she could still –

But none of them had even heard her. Or they pretended they hadn't.

20

'Two hundred quid?' Carol said, derisively. She started to turn away. Sunshine caught the highlights in the fake gold of her hair.

John caught her arm. 'Hey,' he said. 'We're worth it.' Janice could see in his eyes what he wanted – that he wanted it whether Carol had a boyfriend or not.

She grinned up at him as if she didn't understand what he meant, and pulled her arm away; then she turned and signed the equipment log. 'We could do a lot better.' The Biro clicked as she put it down. 'Has he got you on commission, Frank?'

Frank had the grace to look embarrassed as he said, 'No!'

They all headed for the door. Her best chance gone –

'Do you know if anybody's got some spare tickets? I'm after a couple –' There, that didn't sound too desperate. She got the words out just as Frank followed the other two into the hall.

He turned. 'Sorry,' he said. 'Sold out.' He *smiled* at her. Then he left.

Of course they were, she thought as she stared at the door.

Frank trailed John and Carol down the corridor. They were still arguing about the gig, and Frank could see his fifty-quid kickback disappearing out of his wallet before he ever got his hands on it.

That Janice, though, he thought – he'd never really noticed before how pretty she was. She'd looked really disappointed when he'd said they were sold out. He hadn't been lying, either. But being deputy Entertainments Chair had a few more perks than just the odd

21

kickback. If he wanted tickets, he was quite sure he could get his hands on them.

Maybe he should do just that. They were coming to the lifts. Carol was expecting some help with planning next week's regular club night, but he had time to nip back to the lab. He'd ask her if she'd like to go with him. She'd smile – that shy, uncertain smile, so unlike most of the girls around the Uni – and say yes.

He hated that part of it. The asking.

But surely she'd say yes. He was sure he'd felt something pass between them just at the end there.

He was on the verge of turning back when he remembered exactly what she'd said – 'Do you know if anyone's got some spare tickets? I'm after a couple . . .' Not one. Not a few. So she had someone to go with. Well, a girl like her would. Hell, she wasn't even a girl. She was a woman, with a proper job and a flat all to herself and maybe even a family. If he'd asked her she'd probably have laughed in his face.

He shrugged off the last remaining tatters of his fantasy and went into the lift after the others.

Money, Fitz thought: whores do it for money. Writers do, unless, as Johnson said, they're blockheads. Now I'm about to do it for the same reason.

Fitz took his place on the lecture podium. Most of the curtains had been drawn so that he could use the overhead projector. Dust danced in the light that shafted through the cracks in the blackout, and there was a lingering smell of industrial floorwax. He stared round at the students as he waited for Irene Jackson to introduce him. She should just say that, he mused –

'Please welcome Doctor Edward Fitzgerald, Prostitute of Psychology, University of Lowlife'. But she didn't, of course. She'd been Fitz's tutor, once upon a time, and she'd taught him most of what he knew about psychology that could be taught, and a whole lot more besides. Fitz liked to think the teaching and the learning had gone both ways.

But she'd never quite caught cynicism off him – only the veneer of it.

There were a few murmurs, a rattle or two of notepads, and then the hall went silent as the students waited for him to start. They were a bright and shiny bunch, with only a little of the gilt of childhood rubbed off them by a couple of semesters of college life; for all that, they were still a lot more innocent – drugs, booze and screwing notwithstanding – than they'd have liked anyone to believe.

Time for Fitz to go into action. 'When your parents dropped you off at the start of term, they weren't afraid of you disappearing out of their lives for the next three years, turning up changed, damaged, married, lonely, drunk or drugged,' he said. He had them now. Sod your third-hand accounts of fifteen-year-old case studies and clinical notes – give them something that would connect like a fist in the gut. Make them think. Make them *care*. 'They didn't care,' he said. The hush in the hall was almost tangible. 'They were ecstatic to see the back of your bone-idle arses, ecstatic to get the spare room back after eighteen, nineteen years. Can you imagine what that feels like?' he demanded. 'Of course you can't. That's why you're here – to learn about psychology, about life.' He glared at them, daring any of them to disagree with him, to walk out, to put two fingers up at him. Hoping one of them would – that one of them was alive to the possibility that he might be full of bullshit, might not be worth trusting just because he was up on his hind legs preaching at them like a university-sanctioned evangelist. After all, what were evangelists after? Money. What was he, Fitz, after? Money. And no bull about saving souls. Except if one of them had challenged him, he might have done more good than Tammy Bakker and Billy Graham combined. He slapped a page on the overhead projector, but shielded it carefully with the envelope it had come from. 'This is life,' he said. They were expectant now. Maybe they thought he had an answer for them. Sure they did. Sorry to disappoint you, he thought as he pulled the envelope away, revealing a bill. 'Today's post. From the gas board.' He said it as if it were a magical incantation. 'Two hundred and forty quid. Cut off your penis.' That got a laugh – a few shy grins here and there, from students still just a bit embarrassed to be talking about it in public and too gauche even to admit to that. He smiled tightly, colluding with them, knowing that the best was yet to come. Quickly, he exchanged the gas bill for a Council Tax demand. 'I don't pay this one, I can't even vote.' Again, he stared round at them. He was looking for someone, now. If she wasn't there, she was in one of the other universities on his visiting lecturer circuit. She was probably feeling quite happy with herself just now. That wasn't going to last much longer. Not once Fitz had said what he had to say. It was time.

'As my wife consistently reminds me, it really is no

career for a grown-up. Turn back. Go into the light,' he said. They were uncomfortable with that. Not enoug¹. to make them shift in their seats, nothing so crass. But they'd fought hard to get their places, most of them. They didn't want to hear that psychology was a lousy job. Well, they'd find out. Besides, that was just a preamble to what Fitz really had to say. 'But just when I think it's razor blades down Barton Bridge, I get this,' he continued. He held it up so they could see it. There was no harm in that, no confidentiality to be broached: it was typewritten, without even a signature. All that distinguished it was the paper, which shaded from white at the top to deep pink at the bottom. Were any of the students looking discomfited? He couldn't tell. There were too many of them, and they were too far away.

'A love letter,' he explained. Catcalls. A few whistles. 'I don't know her and she doesn't sign it. But someone's in love with me and it makes me glow a little.' He smiled at them, inviting them to join him in his simple pleasure. 'Young, bright, romantic, colourful.' Some of the smiles – especially from the women – were a little uncomfortable. Not that it meant anything. They were probably just thinking about times they'd almost dared do something similar. 'And she's in love with me because she thinks I'm – quote – "special". I can't help feeling special, on a day like today.' Again, he invited them to share his enjoyment.

Time to burst the bubble. 'Then I realise she's a psychology student – possibly one of you.' Now there was real discomfort out there. And not just from the students. Irene was glaring at him furiously. 'Why?' he asked. 'Only psychology students think psychologists are special.' There was a scatter of hollow laughter. That got them all – Irene included – laughing again. But, her aside, it was defensive laughter. They didn't much like it – after all, they were special, weren't they?

Not special enough by half, Fitz thought. Not special enough to stop him tearing into them, anyway – not when it might do that poor deluded young woman some good. 'As a middle-aged man,' he continued, 'I'm entitled to resent your élite, wanky little cliques.' That should really get up Irene's nose, he thought. He shot her a glance. She was scowling. She was thinking of the girl's embarrassment, not the good he might do her. That was Irene's problem – deep down she was a bleeding heart do-good counsellor. She should have learned more from me, Fitz thought. Sometimes you had to dig the knife in deep to cut the poison out. 'She shouldn't,' he said flatly. 'She's too young. But she does. This very normal young woman you've made an outsider. Isolated her. Driven her to want someone like me.' His grin was self-deprecating. He knew what they saw, what they would be thinking – the men anyway: who the hell does that fat git think he is, standing up there, boasting of his conquests? But that would be to miss the point. The point they had to see – the point *she* had to see – was how much worse they must be for her to even consider them. So he made himself out to be the worst he possibly could. All she needed was that single moment of soul-searing clarity that would let her see what she was becoming. He could give that to her. The rest was for her to do. 'A man with debts, for God's sake.' He flicked the bill on the overhead projector. 'This is one passionate young woman, and you cocky

26

little gobshites have missed out. To those men, I say, "Good luck in engineering".' That got a ripple of uncomfortable laughter. They weren't ready yet to consider that they actually might not have the insight to be psychologists. 'To the author I say, "Try the nightclubs, try animals".' The laughter was louder this time. They seemed to think they were laughing at her, not themselves. ' "Try anything that isn't a student." ' Fitz paused, letting the words sink in. 'But in the words of my wife, "Don't touch what you can't afford." '

He stopped speaking. Silence hung like a shroud over the lecture hall. They didn't know what to make of his little tirade. Good, Fitz thought. With any luck that meant they'd think about it for all of thirty seconds after they'd left the hall.

It was a typical Fitz trick, Irene Jackson thought as she stomped down the hall next to him. Go into a hall full of kids – one of them as vulnerable as all hell, assuming she came from this college – and throw a grenade at them. Trouble with Fitz was, he never waited around for the countdown to get to zero.

She grinned to herself. She recognised avoidance when she saw it. As they swung round into the top of the stairwell, she said, 'You arrogant sod. I spend all morning copying Durkheim and you made that up in the taxi.'

They started down the stairs. She held on tight to the slippery wood of the banister. She wasn't old – not by any means, as she told herself fiercely on those mornings after a bad night when she looked in the mirror and saw a face ravaged by lack of sleep and the depredations of time – but she was at a point when she chose to take care. Anyway, she was still moving fast enough to stay ahead of Fitz, and Fitz gasping for a cigarette, as she knew he must be, was no slouch.

'Oh no!' he said, as if affronted at the very suggestion. They got to the bottom of the stairs and he surged ahead of her towards freedom. 'I came on the bus.'

Lord, Irene thought. They *must* be having money problems.

Janice caught up with Irene and Fitz in the Sun in Splendour. They were leaning up against the bar, drinking whisky and chatting like old friends.

'– just wants to get laid like the rest of them,' Janice heard Fitz say as she approached them. That's not true, she thought, looking at him – at the great, comforting bulk of the man, mind as vast as that mountainous body and heart as big as both put together. He couldn't really think that – he would be wrong if he did, and Fitz was never wrong, so he must be saying it for Irene's benefit.

Irene's lips twitched into that sour little smile that irritated Janice so much. She glanced down at the letter. Janice froze. He'd shown her the letter. *Irene*, of all people. It was all right, though – they hadn't seen Janice.

'Well, she trusts you,' Irene said. 'So two years in group wouldn't be wasted.'

It was one of those catty, throwaway remarks that Janice had learned to expect from Irene. Some people never did grow up, they never did get past that adolescent need to score points off people, especially their betters.

28

But Janice didn't have time to dwell on that – this was her big chance, after all. Her chance to talk to Fitz. 'Hiya,' she said brightly.

Fitz glanced at her. His gaze seemed to slide over her – no, through her – as if she didn't exist. 'Sorry,' he said, turning back to the bar and his whisky. 'Curriculum meeting.'

Janice felt her face grow hot. She fought not to let the hurt show on her face – but it wasn't that hard, after all. She'd had years of practice.

'Fitz,' Irene said. She smiled sympathetically at Janice. 'Have you met Janice?' Oh God, Janice thought. She knows. She *knows*. Any minute now the old bag was going to say, *Janice – who wrote you that lovely letter* . . . She felt her palms go sweaty, and pushed them against her dress, willing Irene not to notice, not to say anything: if she said something, and Fitz turned her down, here in public, it would be more than she could bear. Irene stank of whisky and cigarettes, and the smell made Janice feel sick. And then, in the next heartbeat, she realised – there was nothing to worry about. Fitz had been ordinarily rude – that endearing disregard for others that was just his way of saying he knew he was better than them – and Irene had been ordinarily embarrassed about it. 'My lab technician. Joined us this year.'

Fitz grunted something. At her. At Janice. 'Did you mean all that, Fitz?' she asked, relishing the feel of his name coming off her tongue. She could almost smell him – aftershave, whisky, sweat. If she reached out, she could touch his arm, feel the rough weave of the jacket cloth under her hand. Or even . . . even touch his hand.

His face – 'In the lecture,' she added, forcing herself to stop thinking about the possibilities, to live in the moment. Wasn't that what Fitz was always telling them – to enjoy the animal part of themselves, to stop listening to the yatter of the voices in their heads?

In any case, it wasn't necessary. Not now that he'd seen her – that he would turn to her, see the beauty of her spirit that underlay her plainness. Perhaps he'd ask her to dinner. No – not with ratbag Irene around. Slip her a note, then, like a spy in one of the old films he loved so much? Or perhaps he'd come to her – never mind how he'd find out where she lived – like a prince in a fairytale. Yes, that was it – he'd come to her door, perhaps slip the note underneath it. Or there'd be a rap on it. She'd go to answer it – see his silhouette, unmistakable by moonlight, that bulky shadow. Answer the door and –

But he'd turned away.

'Tip for Kempton – two o'clock, Thursday.' He tapped the paper with a finger like a sausage. 'Roxy's Dilemma, twelve to two.'

Racing, Janice thought. He was talking about racing, when she was standing there, waiting for him – wanting him, wanting to make him happy. Happier than that broodmare of a wife of his could. Certainly happier than Jane bloody Penhaligon ever had.

'Grow up,' Irene said. She wasn't taking any notice of Janice either, but then she never really did – not unless some bit of equipment had gone down. 'Kempton's a right-handed track – Roxy's never raced right in its life.' Typical, Janice thought – Fitz had won the students over, so old-bag Irene had to find some way of putting him down. 'No wonder you can't pay your gas bill,' Irene scoffed.

He was looking at Irene. For all she was insulting him, Fitz was far more interested in her than he was in Janice. She's old, Janice thought, dried up, life lived. Got a lot of grey in that blonde, and more if she didn't hit the Grecian 2000. But she's still better looking than I am, must be, if he'll look at her but not at me.

There had to be something she could do. 'Can I get anyone a drink?' she asked. There. That was OK. She sounded bright and cheery, not a hint of despair or desperation.

It worked. Fitz turned back to her. For a second she thought he met her gaze. 'Large Scotch, thanks,' he said, and Janice realised he'd scarcely noticed her.

And anyway, next moment he turned back to Irene, who said, 'Usual, thanks, Janice.'

He doesn't know I'm here, Janice thought as she went to get the drinks. The realisation wrapped ice around her heart. She'd been so sure that if he saw her he'd want her – but what had he seen? Plain Janice, who never could be loved. It was as if Prince Charming had seen a raggedy girl sitting in the ashes by the hearth and never realised what she could be with a little help from her fairy godmother.

Well, she didn't have a fairy godmother – only her sisters, who had always had all the luck – so she'd just have to wave her own magic wand. And when she did, then Fitz would have to notice her.

Fitz had never thought Irene was easy company. She was too damn perceptive, and she was completely unafraid of saying what she thought.

He leaned across the green baize of the roulette table – Zimmerman's had always been Irene's favourite casino – and pushed a small stack of chips onto red sixteen. Glanced round. Saw Irene grinning at him. She obviously thought he'd lost his nerve. The croupier flashed a smile in their direction – some dentist somewhere had made a pile out of her, Fitz reckoned – and clicked the button that spun the wheel. It clattered, the sound almost lost in the noise of fruit machines and people talking. Spun to a stop. Black – the number didn't matter, Fitz had lost. But Irene hadn't. The croupier pushed a pile of chips towards her.

He saw her look at them, calculating how much to put on this bet: whether to make them last or blow it all in one, wild, death-defying – literally, because they both knew that when they gambled they were daring Old Man Reaper to come for them this time – wager.

She halved the stack. He almost said, Getting cautious in your old age, Irene? But friendship forbade it. It was too damn close to the truth, and they'd both know it.

But he wasn't. He wasn't. He piled all his chips into one stack. He saw her looking at him, and knew she knew what he had been thinking.

'You've become a father again since we last went out?' she asked.

Ah, he thought, that's what she thinks it is: one last spurt of wild-oats sowing before I settle into the routine of late fatherhood. Well, she might be right, though he'd have put his money on death first, sex second and mere procreation third any day.

'Boy,' he said, wondering why she didn't know that about him.

'Can't have been planned, surely?'

Bloody woman, Fitz thought. Ought to keep her insights to herself.

'Place your bets, please,' the croupier said.

'Not by me,' Fitz answered. He'd certainly wondered about that – Judith wasn't on the pill, not at her age, but what could have been easier than forgetting to put her diaphragm in?

'But Judith's happy?' Irene asked. She leaned forward and marked black twenty-two.

'I'm happy,' Fitz said. It had come as a surprise to realise that was true. He was happier than he had been in years; certainly than since he'd moved to the new house, and he'd got involved with the police and given up his regular teaching post. 'It was just a shock.' He leaned forward and started to put his chips down. Black twenty-two. Irene was obviously on a winning streak. He could almost feel her grin. Before he took his hand away he scooted the chips across to red sixteen. Bugger the woman. He wasn't going to be spooked by her. 'It's just a shock,' he said, standing back up. 'Sleepless nights, breast-obsessed, burping, farting, turning the house upside-down –'

'But the baby's sleeping through?' Irene knew a straight line when one was handed to her.

'Like a log.'

The wheel whirled till red and black merged into a colourless blur. Come on, Fitz thought. Come *on*. The wheel slowed. The ball rattled and jounced from hole to hole.

Settled.

'Black twenty-two,' the croupier announced.

Irene grinned. Fitz watched, unsmiling, as the croupier raked his chips in.

'That's me home,' he said. He turned and leaned in towards Irene. She touched his arm, and he kissed her on the cheek. 'I could do with the extra lectures, if you can wangle cash on the nose,' he said.

Irene nodded. 'I'll be in touch.' She leaned back against the roulette table. He started towards the door, but she called him back. 'Get him something from me.' She passed him a handful of low-denomination chips – maybe twenty quids' worth, he reckoned.

Fitz smiled. They both knew what she meant. He slid into place beside her and flipped a chip on to the table.

They say you shouldn't gamble with borrowed money, so it was just as well the chips were a gift. Fitz won the next spin. And the one after that.

Moonlight silvered the railway tracks, and the tops of the trees that shielded them from the main road. All was quiet.

The stillness was broken by the roar of an engine. It paused. Reversed. A red van crashed backwards through the trees. Its rear doors flapped open.

A body fell out, then tumbled down the slope. It slammed against a tree stump. The force of it jerked the head back. Moonlight gleamed on naked flesh, on eyes that saw nothing, on teeth bared into a grimace against pain that the body had long since ceased to feel.

The van roared away, and again all was quiet.

THREE

A bell rang.

Judith's eyes flicked open. Bells – she had been dreaming about getting married but –

The phone was ringing. She leaned across and grabbed it, letting chilly air into her nice warm bed. Shit, she thought, but it was all right: baby James hadn't woken up. Someone was saying something to her, but she was still half asleep.

A Liverpool accent. 'Is Fitz there, love?' DCI Wise. UnWise, as Fitz called him behind his back.

It would be. Six o'clock in the bloody morning and it would be someone after Fitz. 'No,' she said, trying to sound alert. 'I'm sorry, he's not –'

The sound of the bedroom door opening stopped her. Fitz walked in, unshaven and rumpled.

'My mistake,' Judith said. 'He's here now.'

Fitz came in and sat down on the edge of the bed. The mattress gave under his weight. He leaned across and took the phone from her.

'Yes?' he said, and pushed a thick wad of notes into Judith's hand.

He stank of cigarettes and whisky. The money was his winnings. He'd long since given up buying her presents on it. Once, she'd have refused it. But that was

35

a baby ago and they needed it too much for her to turn it away. She snuggled back down and fell asleep clutching it.

Jane Penhaligon led Fitz down to the place on the railway embankment where they'd found the body. It was a lovely morning – crisp and clear, with a sky of duck-egg blue above. Too lovely a morning, she thought, to be thinking about death.

Too lovely a morning to be dead, come to that.

But the bloke the signalman had found was dead all right. Detective Chief Inspector Wise came up beside them. Below him, other officers swarmed round the body.

'Young male,' Wise said, without bothering to say hello. 'Twenties. He didn't die here, he's been dumped.' He waved at the trees that hid the railway line from the road. 'Tyre tracks from the road up there.' Alan Temple came over. Wise turned to him. 'You interviewed the railwayman?'

'No sir,' Temple said. 'I've been –'

'Do it,' Wise snarled.

Penhaligon winced. The boss was definitely not in a good mood, and she was surprised Temple hadn't managed to steer clear of him. He might have been demoted to constable, but Temple still had years of experience. Sometimes Penhaligon wondered why he didn't seem able to put them to better use.

As he hurried off and Wise went down the embankment, Fitz came over to her. 'Got any mints?' he asked.

She pulled a packet of extra-strong out of her pocket and flipped one out for him. His fingers engulfed the mint as he took it. 'Nail polish?' he said, and walked off.

Penhaligon followed him down the grassy slope. Somehow he made even that sound like an accusation. Once she would have taken it as a sign that he cared for her. Now it just felt as if he were demanding a reaction. Well, he wasn't going to get one. Not now. Maybe not ever.

She caught up with Fitz. The body was halfway down the embankment. All the signs were that it had been dumped from the top and had only failed to reach the bottom because it had crashed into a tree stump.

They got to the body in time to hear Harris, the pathologist, say, 'Kicked it between six and eight hours ago.' He was intent on his inspection and hadn't seen them yet. He was crouching near the body.

It was – *he* had been – a young man. Younger than me, Penhaligon realised. The thought made her skin creep. He'd probably been quite good-looking – thick dark hair, regular features – but death had turned his face into a blue-tinged mask of agony. He was well built – you'd need regular sessions at the gym to get muscle definition like that – and he had earrings in both ears. There was a spot of colour on his left knee. Penhaligon peered at it. It was a tattoo – a tiny ladybird, complete with spots.

'Asphyxia, caused probably by the electrocution,' Harris went on. He looked up. 'Morning, Fitz,' he said, and immediately continued with what he'd been doing before. 'The power entered the body by the wrists and came out – it has to come out somewhere – down here.' He tapped the corpse's ankles. 'That's the only sign of

37

violence except the head wound.' He waved a hand at the tree stump. 'Caused by this when he got dumped.'

There was a wound at the left temple, and there were mottled rings round his wrists and ankles; but the worst things were the eyes – they stared blindly, mere sockets.

'What about the rest of it?' Wise asked. Even he looked pale.

'The eyes popped with the original shock. The chest cavity exploded with the heated gases.' In the course of her work, Penhaligon had told people terrible things – that lovers, brothers, partners, children, had been killed – but she couldn't imagine using that calm, detached voice to do it. Not when it – when he – had been so young. 'That's normal,' Harris finished.

Beside her, Fitz grunted. 'Naked,' he said. 'Before or after?'

Harris held up a little plastic bag. 'Pubic hair,' he said. 'Not his. He'd had intercourse shortly before he died – that or he's not very hygienic.' He smiled. A man had died, but he'd made a joke and so he smiled. 'Sex and death,' he went on. 'Your favourites.'

'His too,' Fitz said. 'He's still smiling.'

Jesus, Penhaligon thought. Once maybe she would have been amused by that, though it was black humour. Very funny, ha ha, fend off the nightmares with it. She was sure that was what Fitz would say. And now – now she just thought it was callous.

Maybe she was getting old.

'That's *risus sardonicus*,' Harris said. He seemed pleased to have something to explain. 'It's a convulsion. Feature of electrocution.'

Fitz sucked on his peppermint while he took that in. 'You mean if we'd cut to the body when the credits rolled on *Angels With Dirty Faces* we would have seen Jimmy Cagney go out smiling?'

'That's right,' Harris said. His smile widened to a grin at the thought.

Penhaligon supposed it beat train spotting for something to talk about.

'You got any hobbies, Malcolm?' Fitz asked. He didn't usually get on with Harris.

'Hobbies?' Harris said as if the word were in a foreign language that he didn't understand.

'So it's just the work, then?' Fitz asked.

If Harris realised he was being set up, he showed no sign of it. 'Mainly,' he said, without any sign of wariness.

'Drink?'

'Christmas.'

There'd be a pay-off line soon, with Fitz there was always a pay-off, Penhaligon thought. Just then one of the scene of crimes officers came over and handed her a cassette in a plastic bag.

'You wear a wedding ring but you're divorced,' Fitz went on, as the SOCO explained where she'd found the cassette.

She'd have to interrupt them to tell Wise, but it couldn't hurt to wait for the pay-off.

'How'd you know?' Harris asked.

'Hunch,' Fitz said. Harris just looked puzzled.

Penhaligon held up the bag before they could start round two. 'This was strapped to the ankle,' she said.

● ● ●

The gin-and-cigarette voice of Dusty Springfield filled the incident room at Anson Road. *It isn't the way that you look, And it isn't the way that you talk . . .*

Fitz perched against the edge of a desk, smoking slowly, savouring the moment. Photos of the body had been pinned up on the wall opposite, and the room was crowded with Wise's team, Panhandle, Temple and Skelton among them. They were waiting for him to elucidate. Well, he supposed, it beat lecturing to students.

Maybe at the end of the song there'd be a message. But Fitz didn't think so. He reckoned that in the mind of the killer, that song said everything.

It's the way you make me feel, Whenever I am close to you, Dusty sang, and though the words were happy her voice could break hearts.

Fitz glanced at Panhandle. She seemed a little happier now than when he'd last worked with her, but still when he looked at her he could almost see Jimmy Beck standing behind her, see his shadow falling over her face, so that everything she saw became a little greyer, everything she did took a little more effort.

The nail polish was a good sign, he thought. It meant not only that she'd started to take care of herself again, but that she was aware of herself as a sexual being, one with needs that had to be fulfilled.

Whether those needs would ever again include Fitz was the big question.

He didn't have time to ponder it further just then, though. Wise was waiting for him to do his party piece, and in truth he wanted to do it too.

'No sign of constraint other than the wrists, no other

40

signs of violence than incidental,' he said. Wise and the Forensics people would have noted that, of course. Fitz's job was to draw out the implications. 'So what have we got?' He looked around at them expectantly, as if they were students in a tutorial. No response. 'Consenting sex and bondage?'

Temple took the bait. 'A hooker? We didn't find his wallet.'

'There's the post-mortem yet,' Wise said. No one laughed.

Fitz spoke directly to Temple, ignoring Wise. 'If the motive was money, the watch would have been taken. The only things missing are his clothes because he was murdered after sex. Are you listening to the song?'

The pounding I feel in my heart, Hoping that we'll never part.

'Do you think he was gay?' Temple asked.

'Tell me,' Fitz said, wondering if there was any basis in reason for the idea.

'Well, you know,' Temple said, 'the bondage, earrings, tattoo, works out, very muscular – it's a type, isn't it?'

Oh, the fear in that assertion, Fitz thought. He walked over to the picture board, and as he passed Temple he gave his arm a friendly squeeze. 'No, that's a stereotype,' he said. Temple scowled at him. Tough, Fitz thought. It was always tough to break your thinking out of its regular ruts, but Temple could do a better job of trying. 'But yes,' he conceded, 'it could be a gay man.' Temple smiled. 'Could be a woman,' Fitz went on. The smile died on Temple's lips. 'Whichever, he knew his assailant. He undressed himself and got shackled with care – otherwise there'd be bruising.'

'Why electricity?' Panhandle asked.

Fitz grinned. Good old Panhandle – she always did ask the right questions. Unfortunately, he didn't have the answer to that one. 'Execution,' he said, as if he meant it. 'Broker for Powergen shares that took a nosedive?' he went on, all deadly serious, and was rewarded with a few laughs from around the room. But there were a few points left to make. 'Revenge? Probably. Sweet? Definitely.'

He looked at Panhandle. She'd wanted revenge. She'd taken it too, shoving that gun in Beck's mouth. Bastard had deserved it, for sure. But when it came to it, she hadn't been able to pull the trigger. Had not, in fact, loaded the gun. But Jimmy hadn't been able to live with the memory – not of that, not of how he'd raped her: a chain of revenge, then, since Beck had raped her because – he said – she'd made him feel bad over Bilborough's death. In the end, he'd killed himself. Panhandle had got her revenge, but it was far from sweet. He could see her thinking about it – that flicker of the eyelids, the slight tensing of the jaw muscles, the sudden inward movement of the arms, crossing over the body protectively. If he could have taken that pain from her, he would have. As it was, he couldn't even change the subject.

'But it wasn't personal,' he went on, so quickly that he knew no one would even have noticed the pause. 'The song's an epitaph, but not for this lad.' He tapped a picture that showed the body up against the tree stump. 'The body was dumped without dignity. The killer wanted us to know how unimportant he was.'

There was silence while the team considered that.

Wise turned to Skelton. 'How're we doing with Missing Persons?' he asked, breaking the tension that had filled the room.

'Nothing to match locally,' Skelton said. 'They think it might be too early –'

'It was too early for Shergar last I asked,' Wise snapped. 'Tell 'em to shift their arses.' He turned to Temple. 'Put out a general description. Press release. The usual.' He paused for a moment. 'Get a picture round to the sex shops, the gay bars – see if anyone saw him with someone.'

Suddenly everyone in the room was moving, getting on with it, doing the job but refusing to get involved. There was little for Fitz to do, now, until they turned up more information for him to work on. He pulled his packet of cigarettes out of his pocket, but before he could light up Wise came over.

'Have you been drinking?' the DCI demanded.

Where the bloody hell did that come from? Fitz wondered. 'Strangely, no,' he said, knowing he sounded defensive.

'You fancy one?' Wise asked.

Fitz, totally wrong-footed, could only follow Wise into his office.

Wise was a big man, shorter than Fitz, and nowhere near as heavily built, but still big by anyone's standards. He stomped over to his filing cabinet, yanked open a drawer and took out a bottle of Scotch and two glasses. It was a brand-name blend, worth drinking only if nothing better was available, in Fitz's opinion. But at least Wise poured generous measures.

Fitz knocked his back – it didn't deserve better. Wise

43

gulped maybe half of his, then stood holding his glass, giving Fitz plenty of time to survey the office. He'd been in there plenty of times before, but he'd never bothered to scrutinise it, there'd never been any need. But this was clearly personal, and so now he became interested in the personal imprint Wise had left on the room.

There were a couple of commendations from the Police Federation; a framed photo on the desk – that would be his family, Fitz thought, though he couldn't see the picture; a couple of trophies for darts – he'd made second and third, never first; a photo showing a younger and fresher-faced Wise, without the beef or the beard, graduating from training in the sixties – hair like that and he still has the photo on the wall, Fitz thought. Then there was the jacket thrown over the back of the chair – a cheap jacket, with a scattering of dandruff on the collar and obviously past the time it should have been replaced.

The jacket, in a lot of ways, was the thing that interested Fitz the most. For all the flak the government had taken about police pay, a DCI must be on a reasonable salary, he thought – reasonable enough for Wise to buy better clothes than that, at any rate. So, either Wise was stretched financially or he'd never quite got used to making it up through the ranks. He drove a Volvo, nothing flashy there. Maybe he'd gone for the big house and now he couldn't make the mortgage; but Fitz had never heard him complain about interest rates or negative equity. No, Fitz reckoned that DCI Wise was nowhere near as secure in his rank as he liked to make out. For all his years of service, he couldn't quite believe he deserved the money, and that it wouldn't suddenly be taken away from him. Unless, of course, it was his family overspending, bleeding him dry. Fitz dismissed that. If Wise had had problems in that direction he'd have bitched about it before now.

Wise took another sip of Scotch. 'It's my wife,' he said at last. 'Thinks I've got a bit on the side somewhere.' He finished the Scotch and looked at the glass as if considering pouring another. Not on duty, you won't, Fitz thought. 'She's completely obsessed with it,' he said. 'She's on at me in the mornings, she's on at me when I get home, smelling me clothes, rifling me pockets, checking me bank stubs.' His Liverpool accent got stronger and stronger the more upset he got. 'I don't know when she thinks I've time to poke around.' He glared at Fitz as if daring him to come up with an example. 'She's off her bleeding trolley.' He paused, considering the glass again. 'Now she's packed me bags and hoofed me out.' He thumped the glass down on the desk. 'It's my bloody mortgage!'

'B & Q,' Fitz said.

'What?' Wise seemed genuinely puzzled.

'In your last job, that was your nickname,' Fitz said.

'It was never,' Wise retorted.

He was right. Fitz was fishing. He knew nothing about Wise's previous job, but he wanted to see the man's reaction. Besides, the joke he'd just thought of was far too good not to use. 'B & Q – DI Wise. Handyman, helps himself.' He stared at Wise, and the other man met his gaze. 'Every career woman's dream.'

That got him. Two spots of colour appeared on his cheeks. 'I am telling you now, I'm the only bloody monogamist –'

45

'The legend's prospered. It's followed you here,' Fitz cut in.

'– the only monogamist I've ever worked with,' Wise shouted over the top of him. He took a deep breath, and when he spoke again he was at least superficially calm. He leaned forward on his desk. 'I've had chances. I've had offers – more stripes I got, more offers I got – but I've played it straight down the line till it bleedin' choked me.'

All right, Fitz thought. That much heat, generated so quickly – maybe he was telling the truth. But even if he was, he had to have done something to make his wife unhappy: maybe not infidelity, but something, if it was only boring her half to death. Fitz could imagine that.

'You want my professional advice?' he asked.

Wise grinned sourly at him. 'Well, I'm not asking you as a married man, am I?'

Charmed I'm sure, Fitz thought. He pulled out a business card and thrust it at Wise. 'You pay the going rate. Fifty an hour. We sit –'

'Fifty!' Wise said, clearly shocked. 'On your way!'

'That's a call-out fee for a plumber,' Fitz said, narked. 'We're talking about your marriage, you miserable sod.' He glared at Wise, and when the other man neither spoke nor looked away, he carried on. 'We sit down, look at the facts, two columns. Twenty spaces either side.' An expression Fitz couldn't read passed across Wise's face. Fitz wasn't used to being unable to figure out what people were thinking, but he was up and running now. This was the pitch he used when clients came in for an exploratory meeting. 'Twenty good points, twenty bad,' he said. 'And that's where we start talking from. You'd be amazed how many people struggle to get to twenty.'

'It was you,' Wise said. He sounded shocked. Hurt even.

Fitz stared at him, baffled. Someone knocked at the door, then entered without waiting to be asked.

'Get out,' Wise snapped. He turned back to Fitz, and again there was that bewilderment in his voice. 'That's what she said – twenty good points, and she got to four.'

'Who did?' Fitz demanded: but he was only buying thinking time. It didn't matter who it was, it was obviously one of his patients.

Wise picked the picture up off his desk. Wise's face smiled out of the photo. Next to him there was a brunette woman, not pretty, but more than capable of making herself attractive. 'She did,' he snapped. 'Rene bloody Wise.'

'Oh shit,' Fitz said.

'Fifty an hour?' Wise snarled. 'Up your arse, son.' He glared at Fitz, who couldn't quite meet his gaze. 'You're fired – sling it. Do one!'

There was nothing to say. So, just for once, Fitz said nothing at all.

It isn't the way that you look, And it isn't the way that you talk . . .

The song filled up Janice's tiny bedroom, with its comfy clutter of cushions and stuffed animals and the toys she'd never been able to bear to throw away. It was the kind of room her mum had always wanted her to have, a real girl's bedroom, full of little feminine touches, like the ribbons holding back the rosebud-covered curtains, and the sweet little dishes of pot pourri.

She'd never played the record in here before: she'd

47

always kept it for her special place, the special times when she would think about the past.

But tonight was special. Tonight, Fitz would be thinking about her, and so she needed to play the song.

She sat on the edge of her bed and brushed her hair. A hundred strokes, just like Mum had made her do when she was little. As she brushed, she looked at the pictures of Fitz lying on her bed. She'd moved her soft toys to make room for them. Fitz in the newspapers – the so-called Bonnie and Clyde case; Albie Kinsella who'd knifed Fitz's boss; that weird cult who'd killed a girl. There were certainly some peculiar people around, Janice thought.

She put the brush down and got her lipstick out. Cherry Flame, it was called, same as Nina wore. She applied it carefully, just as Nina would. Mustn't smudge, mustn't think about Fitz while she was doing this, mustn't let her hand shake.

But how could she not think of Fitz, when she knew he was thinking of her? Oh, not by name, perhaps. But he was thinking of her all the same, just as he had been when he'd received her first letter. Just as he had when he'd given his lecture to all those cocky students.

And Janice was going to make sure he kept on thinking about her.

FOUR

Judith had had enough. Really enough. They had had yet another embarrassing scene in the supermarket – not enough cash, Switch card debit refused. In the end she'd written a cheque and hoped that Fitz's pay from the university would clear before it did.

So now here they were, back home after yet another silent, seething car ride. It was amazing how it could be a grey, windy day, amazing how deep the green of the rhododendron near the front door could be, when all she could see was the white hot blaze of her anger.

She hauled shopping out of the back of the car and dumped it on the ground. Slam, there went the vegetables. Bang, that was frozen stuff. Whack, booze. Fitz's booze that they couldn't afford anyway.

Especially now he had been thrown off the case he'd been working on. And he had the gall to stand there, gently rocking James in his swing-seat as if nothing had happened.

'That's the only regular income you've achieved,' Judith said, heaving another bagful of groceries out. She was breathless, though whether with anger or the exertion she wasn't quite sure. 'Crime,' she went on. The postman arrived on his bike, but Judith ignored him. 'Regular crime. It shocks me. It appalls me, but it's paid the mortgage.' The postman tried to pretend he wasn't listening as he sorted their mail out from the stack. 'I must be the only woman in the country who sits up for *Crimewatch* with a calculator.'

'Is it my fault I screwed up my benefactor's marriage?' Fitz asked the world in general: that would be because he couldn't quite meet her eyes, Judith thought. 'No, I was trying to earn the M word.'

The postman shoved some letters into Fitz's free hand. He had the good grace to look embarrassed.

Judith stared at baby James. His eyes were chocolate buttons, and he had a thatch of dark hair. There was a scum of dried milk at the corner of his mouth. She felt a rush of tenderness towards him.

'We can't afford him unless I go back to work,' she said, brutally.

'Oh, the joy in that,' Fitz said. He bent over the chair and coochie-cooed James under the chin. 'You were a miracle to save our marriage. What are you now? Three months? Three months, she's turned you into a weapon –'

'Oh, for God's sake,' Judith cut in; but she knew it was true, though no more true for her than it was for him.

'I let her down, she can take it because she's learned the hard way,' Fitz said to James. 'I let you down – I let an infant down – it's "How low can you get?" ' He glanced at Judith. She schooled her face to passivity. 'Hostage shielding,' Fitz went on. I'm not reacting, Judith thought. I'm not – 'This is Saddam Hussein supervising your formative years, kid –'

'Don't you dare!' Judith snapped. She grabbed the

swing-chair off Fitz and left him to follow her in, shopping, post and all.

Mark Fitzgerald was sitting on the loo reading the new issue of *Viz* when his parents came in. They'd been arguing again. He could tell by the sound of their footsteps: his mother's light and rapid, not stopping for anything or anyone; his father's ponderous, slamming into the floor with all his huge weight behind them.

Mark ignored it. He'd long since learned there was no point in worrying about them, and anyway, they did it all the time.

His mobile phone rang. It was Neil, wanting to know if he could swap and do the afternoon shift.

'Yeah,' Mark said.

Before he could say anything else the loo door swung open. His father stood framed in the doorway, blocking out most of the available light. 'Are you joking?' he demanded. Mark moved the copy of *Viz* he'd been reading to cover himself. Fitz turned and called into the kitchen. 'Are we subbing him for this?'

'Do you mind?' Mark said, and kicked the door shut.

He went back to the *Fat Slags* and tried to ignore what his parents were saying about him. It was impossible, though, they were standing right outside the door. Anyway, they couldn't have cared much whether he heard them or not; when he was a kid at least they'd gone into the next room before they'd torn into each other.

'It's no wonder we're skint,' Fitz said. So the row had been about money, Mark thought. So what else was new. 'A penis extension for a nineteen-year-old boy is

51

not judicious housekeeping, Judith.'

'It's Mark's phone,' his mother said. 'He pays for it.' Mark wondered who she was defending, him or herself.

'He can't string a bloody sentence together and he gets a mobile phone?' Thanks, Dad, Mark thought. And then: he doesn't really mean it. But it still hurt. 'Since when does he get a mobile?'

'Since he got a job,' Judith retorted over the sound of plastic bags rustling.

'Job!' Fitz sounded incredulous. That was OK though, Mark would just have to show him. He flushed the toilet, then pulled his pants up.

'Since he started paying board on a regular basis,' Judith said. 'With that and Katie's paper round, we're just about managing.'

Mark went out into the hall. He walked straight past Fitz – he couldn't bring himself to look at him.

'With no conscience and your looks it can only be drug dealing,' Fitz said.

Mark ignored him and headed towards the stairs. Judith picked up the shopping. He knew he ought to help her, but he just couldn't be bothered. Dad knows nothing, he thought. He's got a bloody doctorate in psychology, but he knows nothing.

As he went upstairs he saw Fitz follow Judith into the kitchen. They didn't bother to shut the door, so he heard her clearly when she said, 'Of course, you wouldn't have noticed how depressed he was at not having a job –'

She knows nothing, either, Mark thought. He went into his bedroom, sprawled on his bed and put his headphones on. Anything to avoid listening to them.

● ● ●

Fitz flicked through the post. Judith was banging cans of food around as she unpacked them onto the kitchen table. She said something, but he didn't catch it.

All his attention was on the blue envelope he'd found tucked between two bills. He slit it open. A sheet of paper, pink gradually fading to white, fell out. The letter was typewritten, so it took him only a moment to read, a moment more to understand.

He left the kitchen at a dead run, heart pounding.

Judith shouted something at him. He ignored her.

Penhaligon walked down the corridor of Anson Road police station next to Fitz, heading for DCI Wise's office.

It was almost like old times, she thought. Her and Fitz together, his comforting bulk beside her, working out ways to force her superiors to listen to him. They were good together – a good team, at any rate.

Only there were one or two significant differences that stopped it being quite like old times. She didn't much want to think about it, so she said, 'Does she write often?'

'Couple of times,' Fitz answered. Light glinted on his watch, on his wedding ring. 'First earlier this week,' he said. 'Purple prose, romantic bull.' He paused, scowled. She knew that scowl well. She'd thought it made him look like he was sucking lemons, and found it endearing. So much for that. 'Now this,' he said.

'How'd you know she's a student?' she asked, not wanting to remember the things that had endeared him to her.

'Doctor Fitzgerald.'

'She could be a patient,' Penhaligon said. Just because Fitz was mostly right didn't mean he was infallible, as Penhaligon had found to her cost.

'Patients don't write thank-you letters, they send you hate mail for loosening the nuts.' He looked at her, that sardonic glance that told her she was being set up. 'Once they're better – once you've made them better – they'd rather you never existed. Bit like you, Panhandle.'

Bloody cheek, Penhaligon thought. 'So you've made me better?'

'That's what I'm guessing,' Fitz said. 'You don't return the calls.'

Guess again, Fitz, Penhaligon thought. She'd been right, he wasn't infallible. She speeded up. The neat plait in which she generally wore her hair these days bobbed against her back.

Fitz matched her stride for stride until they came to Wise's office. He waited to one side as she knocked on the door and then went in without waiting for a reply.

Wise was on the phone. He was hunched over his desk, and the knuckles of the hand clenching the handset were white. 'How is it my fault that you've bumped the car, Rene?' he demanded.

So that was why he'd been so ratty lately, Penhaligon thought – trouble at home. 'Sorry, sir,' she said. Wise turned to her. 'It's Fitz.'

'Show him the door.' Wise went back to his conversation.

'It's important, sir,' Penhaligon insisted. 'This is new stuff.'

Wise nodded. 'Look, I've got to go,' he said into the phone. 'No, I'm not making it up –'

Penhaligon backed out of the room. As she did so, she noticed a couple of holdalls in the corner of the room. A soap bag poked out of one.

About as bad as it gets, then, she thought, and closed the door on DCI Wise's argument.

Fitz knew what they were thinking as Panhandle read out the letter. Fat git, how the hell did he get some girl to fall for him like that. He stared around at the team gathered in the incident room. Maybe those weren't their exact thoughts, but he knew they were close. He took a long drag on his cigarette and watched the blue smoke wreathe the air. What the hell did their opinion matter anyway?

' "I think I love you most because, inside, we're the same kind of person," ' Panhandle read from the photocopy she had made. Wrong, Fitz thought. I've never lost my grip on reality to this extent. ' "We do ourselves down all the time. I wish you wouldn't, because it upsets me. You're a good man and you should learn to like yourself –" '

'And this is an intelligent woman,' Wise put in. Fitz glared at him.

She was wrong of course. Fitz liked himself well enough. Surely he did. It was other people he some-times had the problem with.

' "– I know you notice me and pretend not to," ' Panhandle continued as if she hadn't been interrupted. Who is she, Fitz wondered. She obviously thinks she's in a position where I might see her. He tried to think back over all the lectures he'd given recently. Who'd been in the front row? Whose body language was just a bit too open, a little too emphatic? Had anyone brushed past him or made an excuse to speak to him? No one came to mind. ' "I just wish I could bring you out of yourself because I know we could love each other more than anyone could ever imagine." '

Panhandle was making a good job of the reading. Her voice was slightly husky. He couldn't help but remember how she'd sounded in the night, and in the morning when she'd woken with the sun in her eyes and striking red-gold off the highlights in her hair. She wouldn't look at him, or at any of the others. He wondered how much of this she'd felt in all the long time they'd known each other before they'd become lovers. He knew he'd felt something like it – the desire to help her become the most she could be, at least.

Panhandle paused. When she started reading again, her tone was slightly harder. ' "The man who came round for dinner's not my type at all. They're all too cocky for my liking." ' Fitz stared at the pictures on the wall – the body with its stigmata, livid against the white flesh. The identifying marks. ' "Two earrings and a ladybird tattoo on his knee." ' Panhandle stumbled. Wise's head jerked up. His gaze found the picture. Fitz smiled to himself. He took a drag on his cigarette. ' "But he keeps pestering me and saying we're right for each other, and I keep saying different. He's called Steven Lowry." ' She stopped speaking.

There was dead silence for a moment.

'Bloody hell,' Wise said.

'She's your murderer,' Fitz agreed. Now the silence

was electric. It lasted only an instant before a buzz of conversation started.

Wise took the photocopied letter from Panhandle. 'Where's the original?' he asked.

Temple held up a polythene bag containing the original letter and its envelope. 'Here,' he said.

'So yours are the only other prints?' Wise asked Fitz. He ran his hand through his hair.

'And mine, sir,' Panhandle said.

Wise nodded, then turned back to Temple. 'Get it dusted.'

He stood for a second, obviously considering his long-term strategy.

As the rest of the team dispersed to add this new information into the investigation, Panhandle went over to Wise. Fitz hesitated, then followed her. 'Fitz thinks she's one of his students,' she said.

'A student,' Fitz corrected. 'I don't have students of my own as such any more.' He paused, waiting for Wise to tell him where to get off. When he didn't, Fitz continued, 'This letter refers to one of my lectures.'

'Where?' Wise demanded.

So much for the social niceties, Fitz thought. But Wise did look tired – his eyes were shadowed beneath his glasses and he looked pale, as far as his beard would let Fitz see. 'Circuit lectures,' Fitz said. Wise didn't ask for an explanation, so he didn't volunteer one. 'I used the same material for five gigs – Salford, the Met, Queen's; then two in Liverpool. But the postmark's Manchester.'

Wise nodded. 'You happen to see which post office?'

'Brunson street,' Fitz answered. It was right in the town centre.

'That's no bloody use then,' Wise said, as if it were Fitz's fault. 'If she'd used a local office we might have had a chance of tracking her down from it . . .' He let his voice trail off, and massaged the back of his neck with his hand. Five gets you ten he slept in his car last night, Fitz thought. 'Can we see your notes?' Wise asked.

Took a long time to come up with that, Fitz thought. 'The only notes I write are strictly for the milkman,' he said, and smiled.

Skelton hurried over. Wise raised his eyebrows at him.

'Queen's University have a student called Steven Lowry,' Skelton said. 'They've confirmed that his room hasn't been used since yesterday.'

Fitz drew on his cigarette. Wise stared at him as if he were a turd. 'So why'd she kill him?' he demanded.

Fitz couldn't answer that, but he had the perfect diversion. 'Them,' he said.

Wise grunted.

' "They're all too cocky for my liking . . ." ' Fitz said. Wise still wasn't getting it. 'She typed that letter with care. She wouldn't make mistakes,' Fitz explained. 'If Steven Lowry was the first, I'd stick a solid fifty on him not being the last.'

FIVE

Fitz paused in front of the burger bar where Judith had told him Mark was working. He peered through the poster-daubed window. Inside the place was packed with people shovelling their way through burgers and fries and onion rings, and trying not to look too mournful about having been conned into thinking the stuff would bear some passing resemblance to food.

Fitz pushed open the door. A gush of warm air and muzak hit him. He went in, halfway expecting the neon sign to change to 'Abandon Hope All Ye Who Eat In Here'. It didn't, though the instrumental, reggae'd-up version of 'Love Is All Around' was probably warning enough.

The dangling signs that hung at intervals over the heads of the unhappy eaters proclaimed this to be Austrian Month. Best they could do for a marketing ploy, Fitz thought, as he stomped down to the counter, without a major motion picture to tie into. Still, he supposed it could have been worse. They could have decided to do a Victorian Week, complete with Jack the Ripper theme burgers – the MacJack, that's what they'd call it, complete with extra ketchup.

He watched for a second or two. Behind the counter half a dozen staff were dashing around, pulling baskets of fries out of the fat, flipping meat patties or assembling them into burgers, each one precisely portion-controlled. Orders were screamed, though he couldn't see who was doing the shouting.

The staff were got up in red aprons, with ties and Tyrolean hats to match. Fitz couldn't see Mark, though Judith had been emphatic he was on the counter. ('That's quite a step up from slapping a burger, lettuce and mayo into a bun and calling yourself a Meal Preparation Operative, Fitz,' she'd said. 'You should be proud of him – at least he comes by his money honestly.')

The person who was serving was fast – he had his back turned, but Fitz could see his hands fly as he slapped two burgers, a Coke, a milkshake and two portions of fries onto the tray. He turned so quickly it was a wonder the whole lot didn't end up decorating the walls.

Mark? Fitz thought. There was no denying it, though, that was his lad, all right, with his long hair tucked so far up his hat it looked like it had been chopped off, and a smile only just this side of saccharine on his face. 'Two Alpine Kings, fries and soft drinks, enjoy your meals,' he rapped out.

The two lads grabbed their food and moved off without so much as making eye contact.

Shit, Fitz thought. He's doing this ten hours a day for two fifty an hour . . . I'd shove the bloody tray down the ungrateful little shits' throats sideways within ten minutes.

He stepped up to the counter. Mark's expression changed from politely bored to repressed anger.

'Fastest I've seen you move in the last nineteen years,' Fitz said.

60

'Did you want to place an order?' Mark asked. His expression said nothing – *nothing* – was going to make him lose his cool. Or his job.

'Five minutes,' Fitz said, as if it were the obvious response; but he thought, Christ, what happened? There'd been pre-pubertal temper tantrums. Adolescent angst. Rows – about college, about jobs or the lack of them, about the hours he kept and the way he behaved around the house. But they'd always connected on some level. There'd even been a moment last year when he thought they'd achieved something approaching friendship. Mark had stayed when Judith left. There'd been a morning when he'd helped Fitz get inside the head of that murderous bastard Kenneth Trant, the one who'd murdered Joanne Barnes. They'd talked that morning. The one and only real conversation they'd ever had, because shortly after Mark had found him in bed with Panhandle. Not that it had caused a row. Mark had simply shut himself off. That was when the blank look had appeared in his eyes – not for everyone, just for Fitz.

'To eat,' Mark said. There was no forgiveness in his eyes, no warmth. His mouth seemed to have forgotten how to smile.

Fitz scanned the board. He thought about asking for a BSE-burger, but realised that in his present mood Mark would simply take it as personal criticism. Instead he put on an Austrian accent Sigmund Freud would have been proud of. 'Swiss Chicken, Diet Coke, Humble Pie.' Mark didn't laugh. Fitz stared straight at him. 'What time's your break?'

● ● ●

61

She'd done it.

The college was swarming with coppers. They charged past her up the stairs. The people in plain clothes at the front would be CID, she supposed. The rest were in uniform. You could almost smell the urgency coming off them.

She managed to repress her smile till she'd gone past them.

It wasn't till she got outside that she realised Fitz wasn't with them.

Bloody hell, she thought. He still wasn't paying attention. She'd have to do something about that.

Mark could have thought of better ways to waste five minutes – and, he reckoned, he'd be bloody lucky to get away with just five minutes – of a twenty-minute tea break. But he'd promised his father he'd meet him outside: it was the only way to get rid of him. Mark wasn't about to go back on that. If he had the old man would probably have burst into the rest room demanding to see him.

So he grabbed a packet of fries out of the warmer and went out into the square, where a few sad-looking rhododendrons managed to eke a living out of earth covered in bits of paper and fag ends. It was cold. The sky was thick with low grey clouds. He felt the hairs on his bare arms prickle with cold.

This is not going to get complicated, he told himself. Five minutes, tell him everything's OK. Make sure he's OK himself. Back in and I've still got time for a leak before I'm back on duty.

He found his father sitting on a metal seat at the edge

of the square, with the remains of his meal on a tray beside him. Mark sat down and pulled the hated cap off his hair, letting his bush of a ponytail flop down. One look at his father's face told him it wasn't going to be simple.

'Why didn't you talk to me if you were feeling depressed?' Fitz said. A cigarette dangled from two fat fingers.

'I wasn't depressed.' Liar, Mark thought at himself. He stared at the ground. Pink and grey paving slabs in a chequer pattern, only just here they were broken.

'Your mother says you were depressed,' Fitz insisted. He took a drag of his cigarette. Here we go, Mark thought. Man mountain does Sigmund Freud impersonation and I'm supposed to be properly grateful for it. 'It's the baby,' Fitz said after a bit. 'You're feeling pushed out.' He paused, got that look on his face that Mark knew meant he had had one of his famous insights. 'No. Worse. You're the eldest, so it's made you dread your own responsibilities.' Mark ate his fries, trying not to laugh. Or cry. Dad was always right. That's what they said, wasn't it? The police, the papers after every case, the radio show where he did his poxy phone-in. So how come when it mattered he was so wrong? 'The hardship,' his father went on. 'The rows, the frustration, the gut-raking frustration of becoming an adult because this ten-pound suction pump redefines the world for you – yeah?'

What could you say to someone who was so wrong he was nearly disappearing up his own pomposity? Mark wondered. 'No,' he said.

It was too much to hope for that Dad would just

accept that. Mark wasn't disappointed. 'There's nothing psychologically abnormal in it,' Fitz said, so intense he could have caused sunburn. 'It's the sure-as-shit Ghost of Christmas Future. Fill in the gaps, Mark. Enjoy yourself!' He sat back and pulled on his cigarette, apparently happy that he'd done his five-minutes-once-a-year fatherly bit to perfection.

Mark couldn't look at him. I've got to shut him up, he thought. If I don't, I might just hit him. He licked his lips. 'I got Debbie pregnant,' he muttered so quietly he could hardly hear himself over the roar of the traffic.

That got him. Out of the corner of his eye Mark saw him take the fag out of his mouth. His hand was shaking. 'I'm going to be a grandfather?' he demanded. 'Surely not?' He sounded as if he thought he could force the world to be the way he wanted it to, just by saying it loud enough. Mark couldn't think of a thing to say, not in the circumstances. He ran one finger across the greasy surface of his fries carton, and said nothing. 'Look at me,' Fitz commanded. He nudged Mark's knee, hard. '*Look at me*.'

Time to put the old goat out of his misery, Mark supposed. 'She lost it,' he said, suddenly thinking of all those days just after little James had been born – days when it looked as though Judith might be having a breakdown, going on the booze. He'd cared for the baby then, held him, given him his bottle. Just tried to let the wee scrap know someone thought he was a bit more than a bazooka in a family row. And all the time he'd thought: you could have been mine. I could have made you. It had scared him shitless.

But he'd wanted it more than anything in his life.

He turned to his father. 'She lost it,' he said, unable to keep the misery out of his voice.

For just about the first time Mark could remember, Dad was speechless. He flopped back on the seat and rubbed the bridge of his nose. He sighed. 'Now you won't believe me if I say I'm really sorry,' he said. Yeah, sure, Mark thought. He supposed it was better than the way Debbie's parents had reacted. They'd almost come right out and said it just saved on the abortion. Never mind that Debbie had been really pleased to be pregnant. The way she'd smiled at him when she realised he was pleased too. The way she'd smiled anyway. 'Who the hell's Debbie?' Fitz asked. 'Have I met her?'

'Good tits. Skinhead.' And I loved her, Mark thought.

'I'd have remembered the skinhead,' Fitz said. As if you wouldn't have remembered the tits, Mark thought. 'Why didn't you tell me?' Dad sounded genuinely upset.

Because I didn't want you trying to sort me out, Mark thought at him. But it wasn't even true, not really. That was the excuse Mark had used to avoid talking to his dad ever since he'd been old enough to know what he did. What he did to people. The truth was simpler, and just for once, easier. 'You'd have told Mum. She'd have panicked.' It sounded a bit thin. 'She'd have panicked. You'd just buried Gran.'

Fitz sighed. Mark couldn't look at him. Wouldn't. There was a little sucking sound as his father pulled the ciggie out of his mouth.

'And Debbie blamed you?' he asked.

'Yeah,' Mark said. Oh yes – it was the stress, she'd

said. You on the dole, me at college. He'd wanted her to live with him, to get a place somewhere for the three of them. She'd wanted to go home to her parents, even though they wanted her to get rid of it. He'd said, I'll look after you, I will. I'll get a job, support us. You'll see. But she'd yelled at him, told him he was thick, that if he did get a job it would be sweeping streets or serving burgers. That row . . . and that night she'd started bleeding. And now here he was, with the best job he could get – serving burgers.

'She chucked you,' Fitz murmured.

'Yeah.'

'I am sorry. About the baby,' Fitz said. He paused, tapped the ash off his cigarette. 'I'm also sorry that in the last three minutes we've skipped a generation. It's a bit of a *Star Trek* moment for me.' Yeah, Mark thought. Yeah, Dad – look at me. I can make babies, just like you. And I'm just about as bad as you are at supporting them. 'I don't suppose that Wendy hut of yours sells Scotch?'

It might have been funny if there weren't a good chance that Dad was serious, but in any case Mark couldn't raise a smile. 'You won't tell Mum?'

'No – on one condition. You come for a drink with me.' His father was determined. There was no getting out of it. Mark shrugged, the smallest assent he could give. 'Tonight?' Fitz demanded.

'I'm on lates till Wednesday.' It was a minor reprieve.

'Thursday. And we talk.'

'Yeah.' Maybe it wouldn't be so bad.

Dad seemed pleased. 'I know I said enjoy yourself, but for God's sake put some double glazing on the old todger, will you? I've got to go.' He took his tray from the seat next to him and got up.

Mark watched him go, till he got to one of the big litter bins near the middle of the square. 'Hey!' he called. His father turned back. 'I gobbed on your chicken.' Well, it was better than saying thanks.

Dad stared at his tray in mock disgust, then dumped it in the bin. Then he went.

Mark grinned to himself, suddenly happier than he had been in months. Then he thought, bloody hell, the old bastard's done it again.

The police had a bloody cheek, Irene Jackson thought. Oh, obviously they had a job to do, and everyone wanted to see the murderer caught as quickly as possible. But the way they did it! They never asked when they could command, never added a 'please' when they could demand. And Fitz was with them, obviously relishing every moment of it.

She sat with the rest of the psychology faculty – from the Dean right down to Janice the lab technician – in the Senior Common Room. The fat policeman was talking. Now, what was his name again? Irene asked herself. Wise, that was it. There might be a time when she needed to talk to him, and she was damned if she were going to be at a disadvantage.

'We'd like to speak to anyone with details of Steven's whereabouts – dates, nightclubs, social events – last night the 13th,' Wise said. He had a Scouse accent. Irene wondered idly how he'd ended up in Manchester. 'Any students acting strange, emotionally disturbed, unusual behaviour –'

'Well, that's half of them,' the Vice-Chancellor cut in *sotto voce*.

'– anything out of the ordinary. We need your help.' Wise raised his voice just enough to shut down any further conversation.

It would be the ones who were upset they'd want to see, and never mind that being disturbed at a time like this was a perfectly normal reaction to the situation, Irene thought. It was the ones who were acting as if nothing had happened that really needed looking at – either as suspects or for their own good. 'Well, that's bloody nonsense,' she said. 'I object to sending emotionally disturbed students for interrogation, Inspector.' She paused, hoping someone would back her up. 'You bugger 'em up and send 'em back and we've to deal with it.'

Wise stared at her. 'Doctor Fitzgerald has given us reason to believe the killer might strike again.'

Irene's gaze sought Fitz out from the crowd of police. She glared at him. Just for a moment, he was the enemy. 'On what grounds?'

At least he knew better than to bullshit her. 'A strong guess,' he said.

All right, Irene thought. All right. She'd back a guess from Fitz against another psychologist's solidly grounded fact most days. She supposed this would have to be one of them.

After the meeting, Janice made herself a cup of tea in her workroom. She could hardly keep the smile off her face. He was right, he was right. He'd worked it out, paid attention to all the little signs and clues she'd scattered for him.

She fished the teabag out of her mug. Soon, she thought – one day my prince will come. And then you'll see how much I love you.

Frank Weetman was in trouble and he knew it. Taking Steve's essay to use instead of his own had seemed like a good idea just a few minutes ago, but there were coppers in Steven's room. He paused at the door.

A voice from inside said, 'He wasn't always unlucky then?' and someone laughed.

I've got to do this, Frank thought. If I don't, I might as well give up. He knocked at the door.

A police officer opened it. Frank started to go in, but couldn't quite bring himself to do it. There were half a dozen police in there. Steven had never been tidy – got too much stuff to be tidy, he used to say, waving at the heaps of books and CDs and magazines that littered the room, and hoping you'd not notice the piles of dirty clothes he'd not had time to push under the bed – but the police had made the place look as if a typhoon had hit it.

Frank stared at them all, crammed into Steven's place like they owned it. And then he thought, well, he's not coming back now, is he? They were all looking at him, and he knew he didn't have time to get upset.

'I'm a mate of Steven's,' he said to the one that looked the oldest and the most in charge. No one said anything. 'He's got one of my essays . . . well, had,' Frank explained. They still didn't get it. 'The essay's still in here,' he said. God, they were all still looking at him.

'Yeah?' said the copper. 'So?'

'I need it back or I'm off the course,' Frank said. It was half true. The essay deadline was Friday, and nothing that had happened was going to change it.

'Were you two good mates, then?' the copper asked.

Frank nodded. The copper smiled. 'I'm DC Temple,' he said. 'You mind having a word with my boss?'

Frank nodded again. 'But my essay?'

'Get it,' Temple said. 'Just don't touch anything else, OK?'

He pushed his hair back out of his face. Christ, he thought. My hand's shaking. If I'm nervous they'll think I . . . but that was ridiculous. He hadn't done anything. He hurried over to Steven's desk and leafed through a pile of papers he found there. There was the essay. He might not even have to retype it. He picked it up and waved it at Temple. 'This is it, OK?' he said.

Temple nodded and started out the door. Frank trailed after him and they went down to the small lecture theatre. There were two men sitting at the front of the tiered rows of seats – Doctor Fitzgerald and a police officer who would have looked big if he'd been standing next to anyone else.

Temple spoke briefly to them, then left.

'Come over here, son,' the police officer said. 'I'm DCI Wise. There's nothing to worry about – we just want to ask you a couple of questions, got me?'

I've nothing to worry about, Frank thought. I've done nothing. But he wished he could be anywhere else. He walked forward, clutching his essay.

'Let's see,' Doctor Fitzgerald said. Frank stared at him. 'Oh come *on*,' he said. He gestured at the essay. 'What are you afraid of?' He patted the seat next to him.

Frank reluctantly handed his work over and sat down. Doctor Fitzgerald scanned it. He can't be reading it, Frank thought. Not properly. Not that quickly.

The doctor got up and began to pace. 'Recovered Memory: A Testable Theory,' he said. 'You're in Steven's group?'

'First year,' Frank corrected.

Doctor Fitzgerald stopped pacing. 'You know me?'

'Doctor Fitzgerald,' Frank said. He smiled at Fitz, at DCI Wise. Neither of them smiled back at him. 'I've seen you lecture,' he said, turning back to Doctor Fitzgerald.

'So what do you think of me? Am I any good?'

Frank smiled again. 'Great.' He wanted to say, I don't know – I haven't been here long enough to know. You could be shit for all I know. But the others, they all go on about your lectures, about how you kick the crap out of all the reference books.

He half expected Doctor Fitzgerald to pick him up on it. Wasn't that what all the newspapers said? That he seemed to get right inside people's brains? Criminals' brains. But he didn't seem to be inside Frank's brain, because he didn't notice a thing.

'So this quote here, that you've creamed from my book – "Memory serves fact, not interpretation",' Doctor Fitzgerald said. 'Would you agree with that, Frank?'

Oh shit, Frank thought. What would Steve have said? He blinked. Licked his lips. 'Well, I'd argue it to a point,' he said. 'But it's . . . well, I've used it, so I must agree with it, mustn't I?' He smiled again. His mouth was dry. He forced himself to swallow. They'd think he did it, he thought. Why else would he be so nervous?

71

Doctor Fitzgerald didn't seem happy, but he didn't make anything of it. He flipped the essay across to Frank. 'You can go,' he said.

Frank grabbed the essay. He hurried towards the door. His throat was tight, and he thought that if he didn't get outside quickly he might stop breathing altogether.

'You're a liar, Frank,' said Doctor Fitzgerald's voice from behind him. Frank whirled round. He felt the blood drain from his face. He'd known all along that it wasn't Frank's essay. Doctor Fitzgerald stared at him. 'But you're not a killer,' the police psychologist went on. 'The quote's actually "Memory only serves its user, not the truth".' Frank took a deep breath. 'But that's OK,' Doctor Fitzgerald went on. 'He was brighter than you, but he's dead and that's not much use to him now. And like you say, you were good mates.' What's he getting at? Frank wondered. It almost sounded like Doctor Fitzgerald was blaming him for Steve's death, just because he'd nicked his essay. Frank couldn't look him in the eye any more. He turned away. Maybe it had been his fault. Maybe if he'd been a better friend something would have been different . . . yet Steve was the bright one, the confident one, the one who pulled all the girls and was slated to get a first.

Frank started to go out. 'You don't happen to know who he was sleeping with?' Doctor Fitzgerald asked.

'Carol,' Frank said, 'Carol Barker.' But he thought, And the rest.

It was just like old times, Penhaligon thought. Got a difficult question you need asked? Tell Jane to do it. Got a woman whose child or husband or lover's been killed?

72

Get good old Jane to break the news. After all, she was a woman – she must be full of womanly compassion. The only person who hadn't made that assumption was Jimmy Beck, and that was only because he'd thought she was a ballbreaking bitch.

Well, you used whatever you had to get the job done. Right now, the job was talking to Steven Lowry's girlfriend.

Penhaligon hated it.

She hated it so much she'd even asked for Fitz to be there, though she'd sworn to use his help as little as possible. Even as she'd opened her mouth to ask him, she'd realised she'd come round to Jimmy's way of thinking – too much Fitz, too little good honest coppering was bad for them. But she also knew how much of that was based on her personal feelings. And if she were truly going to use everything she had that would get the job done, she had to admit that Fitz was one of her weapons. Otherwise she really would have been coming down to Jimmy's level.

So they'd gone into the hall where the students were being interviewed. It was vast and echoing, full of officers taking statements and nervous-looking students sitting across from them at the little tables used for exams which had been brought out specially for the occasion.

Penhaligon had broken the news as gently as she could. As usual, it wasn't nearly gently enough. She'd wanted to see the girl separately, somewhere quiet and comfortable, but Wise had vetoed that. Carol was blonde. The pubic hair they'd found was blonde. There was just a possibility that Carol was the killer. Fitz didn't think it was at all likely, not considering how the body had been dumped. But Wise did, and the way he glared at Fitz there was no arguing with him. 'Give her a shock. See how she reacts. She might just cough,' he'd said. Penhaligon had nodded and left, with Fitz trailing behind her calling Wise all sorts of names under his breath. Something had happened between the two of them, Penhaligon thought. She only wished she cared about it a bit more, but it was just another thing getting between her and the job.

So Penhaligon sat with Fitz just behind her, watching Carol Barker cry. Even with her face smeared with tears, she was beautiful – huge blue eyes, perfect alabaster skin and a mouth made for kissing. And bright, of course, though in this place that went without saying.

'How come I'm the last to know?' Carol asked.

Penhaligon didn't answer. How can she be so young? she thought. How can I be so old? She wanted to say something comforting, to squeeze her hand, put an arm round her shoulder, let her know that Steven might have died but there were still people left in the world and even strangers might bring you some compassion. Before Jimmy, she might have done it. But she was Penhaligon the ballbreaker, and she had no time for compassion, no room in her heart for mercy. Carol might be the killer. Being kind to her now might stop her confessing. All Penhaligon wanted to do was close the case and move on. So she kept her hands folded neatly in front of her and said, 'You had a relationship?'

'Yes,' Carol said. She dabbed at her eyes with a balled-up tissue.

'Sexual?'

'Yes.'

'For how long?' Just keep the questions coming at her, Penhaligon thought. Don't let her stop to think. Above all, don't think about her tears – about her grief if she's innocent.

'On and off since the start of the course,' Carol said. Her fingers clenched round the bit of tissue. 'We're both doing psychology and he helped out when I first got here. They're not all like that, the clever ones. Most of them know it and wipe the floor with you.' She was more in control now and seemed almost glad of the opportunity to talk about him. 'Steven didn't. Good brain. Funny. Everybody liked him. I was always proud of him, proud to be with him.' She lost it then, and had to struggle to get the last few words out before the tears came. 'And people said we looked really good together.' She stared at the floor. Her shoulders shook with the force of her sobs.

Penhaligon waited a moment. Then another. 'When did you and Steven last have intercourse, Carol?'

Carol's head came up. Her eyes were wide with shock. 'Is that relevant?' she demanded.

Oh, definitely, Penhaligon thought. But even in her current mood she couldn't bring herself to say it so baldly. 'Is that your own hair colour, Carol?' she asked at last.

If Carol had looked shocked before, now she looked appalled. 'What?' she said. Then she worked it out. 'Oh my God – he's been with someone,' she whispered. 'And you let me say all that . . .' Tears tracked down her face. She didn't even bother to wipe them away. 'He'd been with someone else before he died, hadn't he?'

Penhaligon stared impassively at Carol. You'd better hope he had, she thought at the girl. Otherwise you're our best suspect, and the fact that you were obviously in love with him – too much in love with him to be obsessing over Fitz – may not change that. 'I'm sorry,' she said. 'I really can't go into details.'

Carol gulped back her tears. 'Well you could have been more subtle,' she said. She swallowed hard, then stood up. 'You callous bitch.' She rushed towards the door.

Penhaligon watched her go. She glanced at Fitz. He started to say something.

'Don't say it,' she said to him. 'Just don't say it, all right?' She got up and left, choosing another door than the one Carol had left by.

Outside in the hall she stood leaning against the cool plaster of the wall, feeling her heart pound in her chest. I'm not, she thought. I'm not callous. I'm not a bitch. It doesn't matter what she said, what Jimmy said. I'm just making sure the job gets done.

Aren't I?

Danny Fitzgerald stood in his brother's kitchen making coffee. He was waiting for Judith to come home. He pottered around, setting cups out – one for him, one for Judith when she came home and he could discuss the matter that was on his mind, and one for Katie. He could hear her outside, chatting to a friend on the phone. She was a good kid, like her older brother. It was amazing how well Eddie's children had turned out, he thought as he pushed down the plunger on the cafetière, considering the rows and absences that had punctuated their home life.

Some of that would be Judith's doing of course. He found he was smiling as he thought of her. That smile, those eyes, so like yet unlike his own Marie: but Marie was dead, and Judith was married to Eddie, who did not deserve her.

He started to pour coffee for himself and Katie, but then he heard the sound of a key in the front door and paused. If that were Eddie, he would need an excuse for being there . . . He needed to talk to Eddie about the probate – no, too close to his real purpose; he wanted to make sure Judith was OK – but she was doing too well after her depression, and anyway, Eddie would take it as a challenge; Katie, then . . . now, why might he have needed to talk to Katie?

Before he could think of anything, the kitchen door swung open. Judith came through it, carrying James in his swing-chair on her arm.

She smiled. 'Hello, Danny,' she said. She seemed surprised to see him. And pleased. Definitely pleased.

'Want one?' he asked, gesturing with the cafetière.

'Yes,' she answered. She moved forward expectantly, and he went towards her and took the swing-chair from off her arm. He set it down carefully on the worktop. James smiled windily at him. A fine little lad, he thought. If he and Marie had had children, he thought . . . If she'd not got the cancer when she did . . . But it was useless to wish, and in any case he could smell Judith's perfume . . .

'Thanks,' she said. 'Did Katie tell you Fitz is working?'

77

'She did.' She'd know, then, that he'd come to see her. 'Yes.'

She looked up at him. She didn't smile, not quite. But he could see she was pleased.

The student had it all worked out. As Fitz watched, he leaned across the table and touched the hand of the girl he was with. Smiled. Said something funny. She laughed, then sipped her bitter.

You're well in there, Fitz thought. He knew the student was – knock a couple of decades off, and he could have been Fitz: not conventionally good-looking, with that wary look of the outsider about his eyes, and a quirk to his mouth that spoke of burgeoning cynicism and a sharp wit too readily applied, yet also able to charm the birds out of the trees when he wanted to. Or, more likely, into his bed. And knowing it.

Fitz shifted on the uncomfortable bar stool and dragged at his cigarette. The Union bar was full of similar stories, all being played out to their logical conclusions – success or rejection, true romance or broken hearts, all beginning here. He was suddenly aware of Panhandle's presence next to him. She was wearing perfume – he could smell it even through the stink of old beer and cigarettes and sweaty student bodies. At least, he thought he could. There were tiny gold highlights in her red hair, and even her severe plait couldn't stop the late afternoon sunshine picking them out. And her legs, smooth as silk under the long skirts she'd taken to wearing since Jimmy Beck raped her. But he wasn't going to think about her legs. He didn't dare.

'They're all so bloody cocky,' Panhandle said. She

had her arms crossed protectively in front of her. She's scared of them, Fitz thought. She'll never admit it, but she is – all that testosterone floating around, demanding a response. Scared of it, scared she might respond. Scared she might start something she's no longer able to finish. And, of course, scared she might *not* get offered what she only thinks she doesn't want.

'Yeah,' he said lazily. 'But only at face value. Most of them are just filling in time between spliffs.' He took a drag at his own drug of choice, thankful it was legal. 'Hence the confidence. The sex. By the time they're ready to leave, most of them won't even be able to *spell* orgasm.'

It was supposed to make her laugh. It didn't. 'This is the first time I've felt this old,' she said.

Fitz looked at his watch. 'But not as old as . . . *now*,' he said. 'Scary, isn't it?' Again, he thought she might laugh. Again he was disappointed. She nodded slightly, and looked away. He felt as though he didn't know her, this young-old woman with the impenetrable expression. He'd known her once, though, or thought he had. He still held hopes that he could have that person back. 'Too old for sex?' he murmured.

'Yes,' she said, without looking at him. He looked sharply at her. She must have realised what she'd said, because she added more loudly, 'No!' But they both knew which answer came from the heart.

She needed help, Fitz thought. More help than she was getting from the milksop bloody counsellor she was seeing. 'That's the post-rape Catch-22. Sex'd make you feel normal – if you could pull it off.' He paused. At the bar behind Panhandle, the couple from the table were getting more drinks. The girl put her arm round the lad, touched the small of his back. He smiled at her proprietorially. 'But you can't even start, because you're scared,' Fitz continued. 'So you need to control it, but then it wouldn't be spontaneous, so then it wouldn't be normal.' He let her think about that for a second. 'So the whole primitive shebang's history.' He was right. He saw it in her face, in that sudden flicker of vulnerability that was immediately hidden by the impenetrable mask she wore these days. 'Well, it needn't be, I swear it,' he said, and suddenly realised he'd put more passion into that promise than he'd put into anything he could remember. Behind Panhandle, the couple had somehow progressed from hand-holding and shy smiles to full-scale snogging. 'Course,' Fitz said. 'This is trapeze school to the man with four broken limbs.' That, finally, won a smile, though it only reached Panhandle's eyes for a moment. 'The secret's to hang around with the old fat clever guys,' he said. The smile died on Panhandle's lips, and he knew he'd gone too far. 'I could make you feel like Zola Budd again,' he persisted. 'All you have to do is return the calls.' She wasn't looking at him. She was staring round at the couples in the bar like a child suddenly realising they were missing out on Christmas. 'We'd just talk,' he said, wanting her to be very sure about what he was offering and what he was expecting – though he didn't dare think about what he was hoping. But she wasn't listening to him. 'Jane?' he said. He'd only ever called her that in bed.

Her face was unreadable. 'I don't love you, Fitz,' she said in the end. The words were like hammerblows, breaking down all the hopes he'd dared not admit to, all the dreams he'd dared not articulate. 'I think about you a lot. I rehearse the things I need to say.' Even that sounds as if she's been practising it, Fitz thought. He took a long drag on his cigarette, glad she wasn't looking at him, that she couldn't see his hands shake. 'I do want to talk, but as for that –' she glanced around at the couples '– you're wasting your time.' She looked at him as if she were trying to assess the damage.

All he could do was look back at her, unable even to find the words to hide behind.

SIX

'Two thousand pounds?' Judith said, staring at the cheque Danny had given her.

He sat next to her at the table, hands curved round his mug of coffee. He was a large man, as tall and big-boned as Fitz. He looked, Judith thought, as Fitz might if he suddenly lost a lot of weight. They had the same eyes, the same mouth. But where Fitz's mouth was always quirking into a sneer, Danny's was ready with a smile; and where Fitz's eyes most often held contempt for a world he considered far stupider than himself, Danny's held only compassion.

'The probate lawyers keep tracking small policies down – Mum must have had more underwriters than Lloyds,' Danny said. The humour was one thing he did share with Fitz, though it never had that bitter edge to it. 'Five grand, worth four after the Death Duty and fees.' He tapped the cheque. 'That's Eddie's share.'

Judith still couldn't quite believe it. 'But it's got my name on it . . .'

'I could put it in your husband's name – if you want to see the back of it,' Danny said. He was intense, always so intense.

'But legally?' She wanted to give him every chance to back out. Yet she didn't want him to. She realised, with a jolt, that it wasn't the money she would mind losing, it would be that feeling of someone looking out for her. Of having someone she could lean on. Someone to take up the slack when she couldn't handle things alone.

'Legally it was in my stocking,' Danny said, interrupting her thoughts.

One more time: '*You* are giving *me* two thousand pounds?'

'You married him. You need it more than I do.' The humour was as dry as anything Fitz had ever managed, but unlike Fitz's humour, it was aimed at supporting Judith, not cutting her dead. She found herself smiling.

She sighed. 'I don't know what to say,' she said, not daring to look at him.

'Take yourself shopping,' he answered. 'Don't say anything.' He glanced at her jacket, bright as a kingfisher, draped over the back of her chair. 'Buy something blue ...' he hesitated. 'It suits you.' She did look at him then, and the room was suddenly full of unspoken possibilities. His gaze was on her, those kind eyes, offering so much ... He stood up, got his own jacket from the chair. 'Tell him I called,' he said.

Judith got up herself. 'Well, at least let me try and return the favour,' she said. He was still watching her, his expression intense. 'I don't know – buy you dinner?' She tried to make it sound casual. They both knew it was nothing of the sort.

Katie saved them. She came bustling in – going on thirteen, willow slim, with the confidence of the young and unscarred – and went to the fridge.

'Hiya,' she said to Danny as she passed him.

'I'll see myself out,' Danny said to Judith. 'See you, gorgeous,' he said to Katie, but once he'd spoken his eyes sought Judith, and they both knew whom he meant.

Colin was painting the window frames in the spare bedroom – the room that would one day be a nursery, he and Nina had decided – when Janice arrived. She got out of her red van and came marching up the front path carrying a pot plant almost as tall as she was.

For one moment he was tempted to leave Nina to deal with her alone. He stroked paint onto the wood, white on white, carefully touching in close to the glass. Janice rapped at the door. It was no good. He hadn't married Nina to leave her to deal with everything unpleasant alone. He balanced the brush across the tin of paint and climbed down the ladder.

By the time he got downstairs, Janice was in the kitchen.

As he walked along the hall he heard her say, 'I can't believe you've done all this.' She sounded cheery, like she'd no reason to expect anything but a warm welcome. And after what she'd told him . . . He pursed his lips as he went into the kitchen, determined not to say a thing. Not unless Nina wanted him to.

She was holding the plant, while Janice prattled on. 'You said you'd take your time making your mind up about colours and that,' Janice said, looking round at the kitchen he'd spent the last few days painting. 'You look like you've been in months.'

Colin brushed past her and went to the sink. He wasn't finished upstairs, but he started to wash his hands anyway. Anything for an excuse to stay in the room. He wasn't about to leave his Nina alone with Janice. The girl was a grade A cow, and that was a fact.

'I was expecting you sooner, Janice,' Nina said. She swung round and put the plant on the worksurface. Colin could hear the suppressed rage in her voice.

Janice didn't seem to have noticed. 'Well, I've been working,' she said, and smiled as if nothing was the matter. 'It's end of term, everybody wants something.'

Nina crossed her arms. 'Come to look at the damage?' she demanded. 'He told me. He told me what you did.'

She turned and glanced at Colin. He didn't say anything. Nina was doing fine.

Janice looked close to tears. 'Look, Nina,' she said, 'He doesn't stand a chance unless –'

They did stand a chance, Colin thought. They had to. They'd lain next to each other on their wedding night. In the end he'd touched her, tentatively, on the arm. She'd rolled towards him, and they'd made love. It was the first time they had, ever. She was passive, so passive compared to the way she'd been earlier that it was as if she were a different person. As if, he thought, she'd worked out what she had to do, but then, because he'd refused her, she'd forgotten, or not been able to keep up the pretence. They did stand a chance. It was Nina. Him and Nina. Not something that might have happened in her past.

'You were hoping you'd left a mess behind. Again,' Nina said. 'And you were wrong. Again.'

He'd heard all about Janice. How she'd always been making trouble, telling tales, seeking attention, doing whatever she could to drive wedges between her and

86

Louise, and both of them and their father and mother. If it hadn't been for the look in Janice's eyes when she'd spoken to him at the reception, he might have thought Nina was exaggerating.

'I shouldn't have had to tell him, Nina, *you* should've told him,' she said, all fake concern, as if she really thought she could make them believe she cared about them.

Colin scrubbed at his hands, knowing the little cow hadn't a hope in hell of fooling Nina. Out of the corner of his eye he saw her lean forward. 'I'm married, you're not. That's really eating you up, isn't it?' she said. 'Well I feel sorry for you, Janice, I always have. But don't bring me, or my husband, or my marriage into your screwed-up little fantasies.' Fantasies or truth? Colin wondered. Either his wife had had her childhood ripped away from her, or there was something else wrong. It didn't make him love her less, but it made him fear for the future. 'There's no damage, Janice,' Nina lied. 'Grow up, for God's sake,' Nina said. She cocked her head at the plant. 'And take that with you.'

Janice had been near to tears before. Now she began to sob. She rushed over and grabbed the plant, then ran out with it.

Colin went towards Nina. She was shaking. 'Come here,' he said, hoping to comfort her, maybe even to get her talking.

'Don't touch me,' she said. 'Just don't touch me, OK?'

Janice rushed towards her van. The door to Nina's house slammed shut behind her.

They weren't listening to her. Why wouldn't anyone in the world listen to her?

And the fucking door of the fucking van wouldn't even open. She jiggled the key in the lock, but it was stuck.

The plant slid out of her arms. It shattered on the pavement with a sound like gunfire. Pottery and compost sprayed everywhere. Janice glared at it, then kicked the rootball hard towards Nina's gate.

They weren't listening to her. With everything she'd done, they still weren't listening. Well, she knew exactly what to do about that.

SEVEN

All Janice had to do was wait. She was fed up with being Cinderella. Much better to be the fairy god-mother. So she'd cast her spell, and now all she had to do was wait for Prince Charming to come to her.

She knew it would work. After all, it had before, hadn't it? And students were such know-it-all little bastards, with their big plans for the future and the way they strutted around thinking they could get pissed and stoned and laid and still make it all happen.

Well, Janice knew just how to tap into that. So she pottered around in her workroom, sorting out a few bits of lab equipment, and she waited. She tried not to think about it too much – she had work to be getting on with, after all – because when she did she could barely contain her excitement.

There was a tap on the door, and John Branaghan stepped in. He was just about the worst of the bunch – tall, well built, with dark curly hair and eyes that laughed at everything, even when being serious would have been the saner response.

'Professor Jackson about?' he asked, round a wad of chewing gum.

'Meetings all day,' Janice said, as if his presence meant nothing at all to her.

'She wanted to see me,' Branaghan said. He didn't seem surprised – he probably thought she was going to recommend him for a special scholarship, or something.

Arrogant sod.

'She didn't,' Janice said. 'That was me.' It was time to begin. How better to start than by destroying that arrogance that she hated so much? After all, Fitz hated it too. Hadn't he said so in his lecture? She pulled one of the box files down from the shelf over Irene's desk and rummaged through it till she found Branaghan's essay.

She turned with it in her hand and took a step closer to him. 'Look, I hope you don't mind me doing this,' she said softly. 'It's your last essay – she's going to mark you down.'

She knew her stuff. She was standing close to him. Not so close as to make him uncomfortable, but close enough that he'd definitely get the message. Not the right message, mind you, but the one she wanted him to get. The one he was far too arrogant *not* to get.

'How d'you mean?' He frowned. He was unsure of himself, Janice thought, and unused to the feeling. Good. She wanted to keep him off balance for as long as she could.

'I heard her talking to your group tutor,' she said. 'She thinks you're slipping.' Branaghan looked horrified. Poor little thing, Janice thought. Not quite the genius you thought you were, hmm? 'She'll fail you,' she said, relishing the look of panic in his eyes. 'I'm only saying because you were doing really well,' she added.

'Jesus!'

Janice closed the distance between them. He'd be able to smell her perfume now. It was the same one Nina always used, so Janice was sure it would do the trick. She smiled. Not too much. A little bit shy, even. The cocky bastard would go for that, she was sure. 'She'd go mad if she knew we were talking,' she said. This was crucial. 'You understand that?'

He nodded, looking nervous. He was obviously terrified at the thought of failing his year-end exams. So when Janice offered to help him, he was delighted.

Fitz wept.

Tears leaked out from under his shut eyelids. He clenched his jaw against the sobs that wanted to come out of him. Irene's hand was the gentlest of pressures on his shoulder. He reached out for her other hand and covered it with his own.

He took a long, ragged breath. Another. There's nothing wrong with crying, he told himself. How many heart attacks, how many nervous breakdowns had been averted by a good weep? But that was something to tell other people.

Yet you had to stop crying some time, had to begin to heal or all the tears were for nothing. And the only way to heal was to face the truth. He opened his eyes.

Irene's front room – stacked bookshelves, a swathe of silk draped over one wall, knicknacks from four continents, the remains of the Chinese takeaway they'd just shared – was a hazy blur in front of him. He swiped at the tears that still filled his eyes, and the room came into sharper focus. He took a sip of bourbon from the glass he held in his free hand. It steadied him, as much as anything could.

He'd kept his secret for so long. Not the affair with Panhandle – that he'd shared at least with Judith. But that he loved her, wanted her, needed her. He'd never said it. Implied it, maybe. Thought it . . . maybe it had been such a secret he'd barely even admitted it to himself. And now it was too late. He'd never get to tell her, except as a weapon to make her feel guilty, because whether he liked it or not that's how she'd see any declaration.

So he'd told Irene, who was the only person he'd ever known who could get completely inside his head.

'Judith knows?' she asked gently.

'Yes.' Oh yes. That was the other problem – that look of betrayal on her face whenever the police, never mind Panhandle, were mentioned.

'She knows you were or she knows you are?' Irene persisted. The trouble with her was that sometimes she was just too damned perceptive to be comfortable around.

'She knows I was,' Fitz said. 'She suspects I am.' It was a funny thing, that – Judith had thought he was in love with Panhandle long before he actually was. But by that she meant something akin to an adolescent infatuation, not the deep-burning love he'd had such difficulty admitting to himself. And she'd felt threatened by that, when in fact half the trouble was that he also still loved her, not in the way he once had – which had burned so bright perhaps it had consumed itself – but as one of the threads of the tapestry of his life. Maybe not all the patterns it helped to make were pretty, but pull the thread and the fabric disintegrated.

'And Pentangle?'

Fitz couldn't raise a laugh. 'Penhaligon,' he murmured. 'Panhandle. She was . . .' he paused, knowing there was no point even talking about it if he wasn't going to be honest with Irene. With himself. Yet even saying the words brought the threat of tears. His hands, fingering the rough cloth of his jacket, betrayed him. 'Now she says she's not,' he said at last, and added, because he had to, 'Except I don't buy that.'

'Well, no, you'd be a fool to admit it,' Irene said. He could feel her on the sofa beside him, and the simple human contact helped.

'Too many things got in the way,' Fitz said. 'Bilborough's murder, the rape . . . Beck's suicide was the only highlight.' He wasn't able to keep the contempt out of his voice. 'I spit on that bastard's grave every time his name gets mentioned.' He drew in a long, ragged breath to ward off the tears that were suddenly very close. 'None of it was anything to do with *us* – nothing we'd made happen.' He wanted to look at Irene, to make sure she understood, but he couldn't. The slightest hint of sympathy and he'd be in floods again. 'She's knitted the whole bloody cardigan and put sleeves on it,' he went on. 'She's absorbed the guilt – she gets the guilt, I get the blame.' He stopped, knowing there was one more thing he had to say, or make a mockery of his honesty. 'And suddenly, we've got sex on the menu again.' He couldn't keep the anger out of his voice. Anger at her, for wanting sex but not with him. Anger at himself for hurting, and crying in front of Irene. But mostly anger at whoever it was she wanted instead of him.

'You think she's met someone else?'

He didn't answer, just downed the rest of his bourbon. It burned as it hit, the way his heart burned when he thought of her – of the nail polish she was wearing again, the stylish clothes that were beginning to make a reappearance.

Irene said, 'In the other house, I had a new carpet fitted. Beautiful carpet. Not cheap, but it transformed the room.' Fitz frowned, not seeing the relevance, but lacking the energy even to ask what she was talking about. 'The week after, Clive died,' she went on. 'Two months later, my mother died. Then the publishers – not a very good one – turned down my latest book.' She smiled. 'There was a very simple solution. I burnt the carpet and I've never looked back.'

'Oh, for God's sake, Irene.' It was the kind of irrational twaddle they both derided daily.

Before he could say anything else, Irene pulled away from him and sat up. 'Look, you've got Judith, who's forgiven you, three children with bright futures, and a damn sight more luck than I ever had.'

'It's taken four decades of social science to sound like Esther bloody Rantzen?' Fitz snapped. That's the boy, he thought at himself. If you can't take it out on Panhandle's hypothetical lover, take it out on the nearest target – even if that is the only person you've ever really been able to talk to.

Irene gulped her drink. 'I paid for the takeaway, I can say what I like,' she said. She laughed. So did Fitz, and just for a second it was enough that he still had a friend.

● ● ●

Janice checked her appearance in her bedroom mirror. The black silk dress she was wearing was cut low enough to be enticing without revealing too much. She stroked her hair back from her perfectly made-up face. Dad used to do that, she thought. When he would come upstairs to say goodnight. Sometimes she would lie in the darkness, pretending to sleep. He would come in and sit on the edge of the bed, and stroke her hair in the silence. His hands had been so gentle . . .

But that was then and this was now. She turned from the mirror. The bedroom was neat and tidy. She'd put all her Fitz pictures and cuttings safely away where no one but her could see them. She'd piled all her soft toys on their shelves and the top of her chest of drawers. She didn't want to have to stop to move them once things got going. She picked one of them up, and cradled it in her arms. It was an old-fashioned teddy bear. She'd been given it for her first birthday, so they said, but as far as she was concerned it had always been there, all through the long lonely nights when she'd realised she wasn't like the others.

'Hush Mr Bear,' she whispered. And then, because it was in her head but she didn't want to play the record yet, she began to sing. *'It isn't the way that you look, And it isn't the way that you talk.'* She did a fair impersonation of Dusty, she thought. The clock said two minutes past eight. He was late. Little so-and-so, keeping her waiting, she thought. But she couldn't get too angry, knowing he was going to bring Fitz to her. This time, surely he would. *'I can't believe this is really happening to me,'* she crooned to Mr Bear. It was true. She couldn't believe that she'd finally taken control, and refused to be a victim to all the dreadful things that had happened to her. 'I have to do it, Mr Bear,' she whispered. 'I have to make him notice –'

There was a knock on the door. Hastily, she put Mr Bear back on his shelf and went out, smoothing her dress against her thighs as she walked.

She opened the door. John Branaghan stood there, silhouetted against the dying light of the late evening.

'Hi!' he said. 'I brought you these,' he said, holding out a wrapped box.

Janice took the box. 'Thanks,' she said. 'Come on in.'

She led him through into the front room, and they sat down on the sofa in front of the coffee table.

Janice put the chocolates down next to the folder containing Branaghan's essay. 'You don't mind if I open them?' she asked, grinning like a kid on her birthday. He shook his head. She undid the parcel, to reveal a box of After Eights. 'Oh how sweet of you,' she said. 'My favourites.' But she thought, you tight little bastard. 'Want one?'

He took one, and ate it slowly, never taking his eyes off her.

He really was very good-looking, Janice thought. It was almost a shame that . . . but she remembered Fitz, and the compassion in his voice when he said that she was a passionate woman, that all the cocky little students had missed out, and the words of the song came back to her, *It isn't the way that you look, And it isn't the way that you talk* . . .

Too bad looks aren't everything, she thought, and pulled the folder containing John's essay towards her.

● ● ●

The house was smarter-looking than Wise had feared. It was on a corner, and there were fancy ruched curtains in all the windows. A sign by the door proclaimed it to be the Excelsior Guest House. He hefted his holdall and walked up to the front door, determined to put a good front on things. It wasn't going to be easy though. Not feeling the way he did.

He still hadn't worked out exactly what he was supposed to have done. Rene had said he wasn't fit to live with, though, and she should know.

So now he was supposed to go and live with complete strangers.

He rang the doorbell. A woman answered within seconds, and he wondered if she'd been looking out for him.

'Mr Wise, love,' he said. 'I rang about a room. I got stuck in work, I'm sorry.' He'd told her he was a police officer, knowing it would be easier to get a place, but he hoped she wouldn't ask too many questions. He couldn't believe she'd really want to know that he'd spent his day co-ordinating what looked set to become an inquiry into a serial murderer.

She clutched at the string of beads round her neck. She was carefully made up, and if Wise had been a betting man, he'd have laid odds her black hair was dyed.

'That's right,' the woman said, and opened the door a little further.

'Is the car all right there?' Wise asked, looking back at it. 'I'm blocking the gates . . .'

'Park it in the drive if you like,' she said. She smiled. 'I've no other guests at present.' Something in her expression told Wise she was desperate for the company – for male company, even. It was the last thing he needed. Her smile widened a little further. He hoped – he really did hope – she wasn't thinking what he thought she was. He started down the steps to the path.

Her voice stopped him. 'Actually,' she said. He turned. 'Do you take milk? With your breakfast?'

'Well on me cornflakes, yeah,' Wise said.

'I don't, you see. And I'm out.' Great, Wise thought. 'The Spar shuts in ten,' she said. She came down the steps towards him. 'I could stick the kettle on.' She said it as if it would be a great adventure.

Wise smiled. 'Right,' he said, though he'd hoped to spend the evening reading the paper. Alone. In his room.

She picked up his bag. 'I'll just take this up for you,' she said. 'Oh, and do call me Sandra, won't you?'

'Yeah,' Wise said. He scowled as he turned away.

Sandra didn't seem to notice.

Janice leaned forward, and tapped John Branaghan's essay with her finger. She felt him stare, not at the essay, but at her cleavage. She wriggled slightly, so that her dress – tight and black – rode up her thighs. She'd watched Louise tease a whole string of boyfriends that way. And before every date, she'd come in to the front room, showing off this dress or that one, demanding to know if Dad thought she were beautiful, if the dress and the makeup would do.

Well, Janice could do that too. Janice had. And now John Branaghan was here and he couldn't take his eyes off her. She smiled. He wasn't even the one she wanted, but here he was, desperate for her.

'It's my writing, but Professor Jackson's notes,' she said. She turned to look John in the eyes. They were so close that she could have leaned forward and kissed him, if she'd wanted to. She didn't. She wanted him to come to her – wanted to know that he wanted her, the more urgently the better. 'I copied them. Basically, it's once more with feeling.'

That was nonsense. The essay was brilliant. It was that brilliance that had made Janice choose John. After all, she wasn't going to settle for less than the best, and anyway, the better he was the more he needed taking down a few notches.

'I don't understand it,' he said. He sounded genuinely bewildered. Well, Janice thought, poor lamby probably isn't used to screwing things up. Can't admit to it. 'I put a stack of work in on this one, it's clean as a whistle,' he rattled on. 'If I deserved duff marks for any of 'em, it was the last, and that got an A.'

Well, it would if *you* wrote it, wouldn't it? Janice thought. But she smiled again, and said, 'Hang on, I copied your last one by chance. We should have a look at what she said on there – she's all over the place sometimes, you know.'

She got off the sofa and bent over to search through her bag. He'd be looking at her backside. She knew it. She'd planned it that way.

'She can change her mind one day to the next about what suits her,' she said, and squatted back on her heels. 'She takes some keeping up with.' She heard him come up behind her.

'I really appreciate all this, you know.'

She could feel his breath, warm on her cheek.

'My pleasure,' she said, and paused just long enough to leave what she meant in doubt. 'Be a shame to get in her bad books just because of a few late nights.' She pretended to lose her balance, and her shoulder brushed his chest. 'Sorry,' she said.

He moved forward, just a little, and now they were pressed up close against each other. 'I never said anything about late nights,' he said.

'You've a dodgy reputation.'

'You bothered to find out.' His hand touched the small of her back.

'It gets round,' Janice murmured, looking at him from heavy-lidded eyes.

He leaned in and kissed her, gently at first but then fiercely. His hand slid down the silk of her dress to her backside. His other hand cupped her breast. She leaned into him and started to unbutton his shirt. His skin was satin under her fingers. He slipped the straps of her dress down over her shoulders, then dropped to his knees to kiss her breasts.

She knotted her fingers in his hair and closed her eyes, wishing that the hands moving over her behind and up between her thighs were Fitz's, that it was his mouth, not John's, seeking out all her soft and secret places –

– and yet, she could not stop herself responding, could not stop her hands and lips moving over the iron-in-velvet hardness of him –

– and later, when he rammed himself up into her and she locked her legs around his hips and felt his arms round her holding her and her breath came in hard sharp little gasps and there was nothing she could do but give herself over to the insistent hammering of desire she bit hard into his neck to stop herself crying out, because he wasn't Fitz and she wouldn't wouldn't *wouldn't* give herself to any other man so completely.

He yelped.

'That good, hmm?' he said, and laughed. 'Well, I've hardly even started –' and slammed himself into her so hard that this time there was no resisting and she didn't want to resist the moan that welled up inside her . . .

Jane Penhaligon stared through the window at the street outside her flat. She was wearing a cream silk suit which she had bought specially, and for the first time in months she was wearing her hair down. It fell in a luxuriant red mane over her shoulders.

She looked at her fingernails. She was wearing polish on them. Fitz had remarked on that, though his opinion mattered less to her now than it had before. She wondered what he'd say to the fact that she was also wearing makeup – not much, just a touch of blusher and lipstick, a little mascara and the merest touch of eyeshadow.

If I don't care about his opinion, why am I thinking about what he'd say? she wondered. No doubt if she asked he would tell her. But she didn't want to ask. Did not, in fact, want to go through with what she'd decided to do this evening.

It's a date, she thought. That's all. A meal. A movie. I'm not going to go to bed with him. The thought made her flinch.

The doorbell rang.

Penhaligon took a deep breath and went to answer it.
'Hi,' she said.

'Hi yourself,' Alan Temple answered.

Afterwards, John Branaghan lay on the front-room floor next to Janice. They were both panting, breaths matched, while their bodies caught up with the storm that had overtaken them. They were sweat-drenched and spent. She turned to him and put her hand on the flat muscular slab of his belly. He covered her hand with his own.

It had been an all-right screw – nothing to brag about down the Union, but all right. He hoped she wasn't going to get silly about it, though.

He pushed her hand away: gently enough, but still away. He rolled to a sitting position.

'Thanks,' he said.

He got up and grabbed his boxer shorts.

'Stay,' she said as he climbed into them. Oh gawd, he thought. Here we go – she's going to want to know when we can see each other again now.

'I'd better not – I said I'd meet a couple of mates down the Union,' Branaghan said. He turned away and started to gather his clothes together.

One fuck, they thought they owned you. Wasn't like he'd promised her anything, after all.

Still, maybe he'd better find something nice to say to her. Didn't want her weeping on Jackson's shoulder, after all. Maybe he could tell her the university wouldn't think it was appropriate for a staff member to have a relationship with a student. Yeah, that would do it.

He turned round.

She wasn't there.

'Janice?' he called. There was no answer. He looked around. There was a door at one side of the room. He pushed it open, but hesitated before going in. The room was almost more like a nursery than a grown woman's room, what with the sugar-pink walls decorated with pictures of cute animals and children, and the shelves and shelves of soft toys. Well, he thought, each to their own.

It certainly hadn't made her a bad lay.

He stepped inside. 'Janice?' he called. He looked round, then strode over to the bed and looked underneath it. 'Janice!'

The sound of her laugh came from somewhere, but he couldn't tell where. He whirled round. There was a velvet curtain where the wall should be – there surely couldn't be a window behind it, he thought.

An alcove, maybe? Whatever her game was, he was beginning to enjoy it. He strode towards the curtain. 'Janice?' he shouted. He grinned. 'Where the hell are you, you lunatic?'

He heard a noise from behind him and turned in time to see her emerge from behind the curtain. She grabbed his wrist with one hand, hard. Before he had time to react she'd snapped handcuffs on his wrist.

'Jesus,' he said. The white marks her fingers had left started to fade.

'We're sticking on B-minus, then?' Janice teased. She was wearing a silk wrap now, and as she moved he could see the outline of her breasts under it.

'I thought I was fantastic,' John protested.

'That's a bit of a pattern, isn't it?' she asked. He'd thought she was turned on before, thought she didn't get enough, she'd become so aroused so quickly. But now she was almost glowing with excitement.

He was breathing hard now. Whatever she had in mind, he was definitely up for it.

She tugged on the handcuffs and backed away, through the curtains. He followed. He had no choice.

'Bloody hell,' he said. The room she led him into was enormous. It was lit by row upon row of candles that sent shadows dancing over the walls, which she'd decked out with swathes of white gauze. In the middle of the room stood a black iron bedstead. It too was surrounded by candles. 'You own all this?' His eyes flickered around, trying to take it all in. 'Talk about being taken for granted. Is all this for me?'

She just laughed and pulled him close. They moved towards the bed. He kissed her gently on the lips, suddenly glad that they'd done it once already. Now he'd be able to take his time, to really make the most of whatever games she had planned. He started to push her down on to the bed, but she moved round and he realised she wanted to ride him. When she shoved him in the chest, he let himself fall back onto the mattress.

She picked his legs up and swung them round, so that he was completely on the bed. As she did so, the robe parted just a bit so that he could see she was nude beneath it. He was about to reach up for her when she climbed onto the bed.

She straddled him. The robe fell open, and he stared at her breasts. He reached up to her, but she took his hand gently, then clipped a handcuff on that wrist. The

104

chain on the handcuffs jangled. Oh yes, he thought, that's right – I'm supposed to be at her mercy. Well, he could play at that game. She leant down over him. He smelled honeysuckle and sweat. She kissed him hard on the mouth, then let her tongue trace circles on his cheek. Her thighs locked over his groin, and he felt his hard-on rub against his boxer shorts.

John felt his arm being pulled by the chain, which jingled. There was a sharp click. Janice sat up. John looked at his wrist, which was now cuffed to the bedstead. He grinned, excited by the idea.

'I feel a bit of revision coming on,' he said. In truth, he had an erection like he'd almost never had before. If he could have, he'd have reached for her then and taken her. But that was the point, wasn't it? That he couldn't. That Janice – drab little Janice the lab technician – was in charge now. In control.

She reared up over him, smiling slyly. She took his free arm in her hands, and without saying a word, chained his other arm to the bed. He wrapped the chains round his hands. They were cold. He jangled them. He was held securely. There'd be no getting free till she let him go.

That look on her face, he thought. Not desire. Triumph, maybe. Well, she certainly had him where she wanted him.

Come to think of it, given the set-up, she'd obviously had a lot of men where she wanted them. The thought excited him.

Now, he thought, surely she'll undress me. I'm no good to her with my shorts on, am I?

But she leaned back and round, and lay along his

legs. He stared at her arse, wanting to touch it but not being able to.

'You've obviously done this before,' he said. She fitted an iron cuff round his ankle. He lifted his leg to help her, and she snapped it shut. 'I haven't.' He sounded nervous. God, him, John Branaghan, nervous in bed with a woman. 'If you want the truth, I'm not generally submissive like this, so this should be interesting.' God, that was the word, wasn't it. Submissive. A bit scared even. Not that he wanted her to know that. What if she were into something really alternative? S&M, maybe, with the emphasis on the S? She'd turned again, twisted right round so the thin silk of her robe stretched tight across the curve of her arse. Jesus. Could he get much more aroused without coming? He didn't think so. She tugged at his leg. He felt something rough touch it – rope. She was tying his leg to the bed with rope.

How much longer was she going to make him wait? This was going to be so good ... so good. And then maybe she'd let him take a turn. He thought of her, spreadeagled on the bed for his pleasure, legs open wide, waiting for him ...

She turned back round, so she was astride him again. She was moist between the legs – he could feel it seeping through his shorts. She wanted him. Christ, she did. How could she restrain herself?

Well, she'd certainly restrained him. And now here she was staring down at him. She still hadn't said a word since they'd begun. She leaned over and took a jar of clear gel from the bedside table. She unscrewed the top, slowly, never taking her eyes from him. She had

106

something in mind, but what? He certainly wasn't in the right position for a backrub. Of course, she might be thinking of rubbing it somewhere else . . . he wondered if it were flavoured. 'You like to make men nervous, don't you?' He giggled. Well, he was nervous all right. She dipped her fingers in the gel, and they came out glistening. He thought of licking them clean. Of sucking at her. 'Real dark horse, aren't you?'

'Sshhh,' she said. She smoothed the gel on the inside of his left wrist. It was so cold it made the hairs on his arms stand up.

But he couldn't be quiet. Not when talking was the only release he had. 'All the times I've seen you in the office and –'

'Sshhh,' she said again, as she gelled his other wrist.

'– I'd never for one minute imagined –'

'Shut up!' she screamed at him. Her eyes bulged and her mouth contorted into a sneer.

'Jesus, what did I –' he started. He tasted fear like old copper in the back of his throat. His heart pounded so hard he thought his chest would burst.

'Just shut up!' she howled at him again. She clambered off the bed. 'You lot don't know when to stop, do you?' The candlelight turned her face into a mask of rage. Two spots of colour stood high on her cheeks. 'Fitz is right,' she yelled. 'Smart-arsed, cocky little gobshites.' She was almost in tears. Her eyes glistened in the yellow light. 'He's standing up there trying to tell you things and you're just not *listening*!' A fleck of spittle flew out of her mouth and danced for a moment in the candlelight. Then it was gone.

She stared at him for a moment, as if she was making

107

her mind up about something.

Then she turned and walked away. She disappeared behind a partition. He could see her doing something behind the nubbled glass of its upper half.

Jesus, he thought. What's she up to? What have I let myself in for? He yanked on the chains. Fear made his hands sweat, and they slipped on the cold iron. There was no breaking free, but maybe with the gel he could slip his hands through . . .

It was useless.

Got to keep her talking. If he could get her to calm down, maybe she'd see reason. 'I won't say anything,' he said.

'Shut up.'

'I won't tell anyone.' He tried the manacles again, but they were heavy enough to chain an ox.

'Shut up.' Her voice was thick with tears.

'Please,' he begged. Maybe that was it. Maybe it was just part of the game. Maybe she just needed to hear him plead. Maybe . . . 'Whatever this is about, I didn't mean to upset you.'

'Shut up.'

The hiss of a stylus on an old-fashioned vinyl record started. Piano music, heavy and melodramatic.

'Please,' he shouted. This time, Janice didn't answer. Instead, the vocals started on the record. A woman's voice. Not someone he recognised. *It isn't the way that you look, And it isn't the way that you talk.* Janice came to the gap in the partition. She stared at him, and the look on her face terrified him more than anything that had happened so far. Contempt. And pity. It was the pity that scared him.

It's the way you make me feel, Whenever I am close to you.

'Please,' he screamed again.

Janice smiled sadly as she walked towards him.

EIGHT

Judith lay staring into the darkness, alone. Baby James was in his cot by the bed, and there was a nightlight on for him. But Judith was still alone, and it was still dark.

She hadn't seen Fitz since that morning. He hadn't phoned to say he wasn't coming in. She'd long ago stopped worrying that he might have been in an accident. There'd come a point when she'd realised that was just another way of making excuses for him: and at that point – which had come fairly early on in their relationship – she'd understood that she really did love him. Before then, she'd thought maybe it was just an infatuation. That she could give him up, find someone else, just as all her friends said she should. But when she'd realised that he was never going to change, and that she accepted that, she'd known she loved him – that she would always love him.

After that, there was no point in leaving him.

So now she stared into darkness, past the empty space in the bed where he should have been, and she wished she did not love him. Had not loved him. Could have left him, since that would have been wiser.

A floorboard creaked. The bedroom door swung open. Fitz came into the room, a vast dark shadow in the yellowish glow of the nightlight. He moved quietly across to the bed and lowered himself on to it. The bed gave under his bulk.

He didn't even look at Judith to see if she were awake, just lay staring up at the ceiling. His cheeks were smeared and his eyes looked sore.

'Danny was here,' she said. That was nothing new, but somehow she didn't want Katie or Mark telling him before she did. Talk to me, she thought. We can still do this, if you'd only talk. You'd tell other people to.

'Sorry,' he said. He thumped the mattress. 'Thought it was vacant.' Now what the hell did he mean by that, Judith thought. She thought of Danny, of the intense way he'd looked at her when he said, 'Goodbye, gorgeous.' Of him telling her to buy something blue because it suited her. But perhaps Fitz meant nothing at all, except another throwaway line. 'Any message?' He breathed in, long and hard. It sounded as if he needed to blow his nose.

Perhaps she shouldn't have said anything. 'You've been crying,' she said. He didn't answer, but his tongue worked against his lips. 'Have you seen her tonight?' She didn't want to know the answer, but she had to. She'd been so sure it was over ... she'd thanked whoever it was who'd raped Penhaligon, because it pulled her and Fitz apart. Then she'd hated herself for it. But if they'd started again –

'No.'

'That's why you've been crying.'

It wasn't a question, but he said again, 'No.'

Liar, she thought at him; but she knew there was no point trying to force him to talk. There was silence for a long moment. Then he turned to look at her. He seemed

112

about to say something, but then he turned away again.

'What?' she asked. He said nothing. *'What?'*

'When was it we last fitted new carpets?' he demanded.

Oh for God's sake, Judith thought. It didn't even seem worth demanding an explanation. She sighed loudly, wrapped the duvet round herself and rolled over so she didn't have to look at him.

It would be all right. He was in the back of the van now, with the cassette strapped to his ankle. No one had seen her shove him in there, wrapped in a potato sack to make handling him easier. Janice clutched at the steering wheel with her gloved hands as she drove down the track through the woods. She'd have left the body in the same place as the first one, if she'd dared – that had felt right, somehow; but she knew if she did that she'd be giving them too much. Too much, too fast. Her heart was racing, but she forced herself to drive carefully. The last thing she wanted now was to attract attention to herself.

At least it wasn't far. She found a gap in the trees and backed into it. The sky was dark with cloud.

No one saw me then, she told herself. No one's around to see me now. She gunned the motor. This was the tricky bit. She needed speed, but not too much, and it wasn't easy to judge with the plastic overshoes on her feet. Didn't want to overshoot the bank. On the other hand, she wanted to make sure . . .

She slammed the brakes on. The jolt slammed her forward. An instant later there was a second, lesser jolt as the doors, loosely secured with string, burst open.

113

She heard his body bounce down the bank.

Serve the arrogant little gobshite right, she thought.

She climbed out and went to shut the doors. She couldn't resist one last glance at him as he lay there. The cloud shifted, and moonlight bounced off his pale body, and the water that lay puddled near him. His arms were spread as if he were begging, and he was smiling.

Laughing at her, she thought. Well, it was the last time he'd patronise anyone. She slammed the van doors shut.

She went and sat on the edge of the driver's seat. She stripped off the overshoes, making sure her feet didn't touch the muddy ground. Then she got into the van and started the engine.

It fired immediately, but the wheels spun uselessly in the mud.

'Shit,' she said. She whacked the steering wheel with her hands. She revved the motor, but she knew it was useless. All she was doing was digging herself in deeper. 'Shit!' she said again.

She checked her watch. Just gone ten. She stared out of the windscreen at the path. It glistened wetly in her headlights. It was too damn early. She knew she should have left it till a bit later, but she'd thought she might be more noticeable then. If someone came . . .

A dog barked in the distance. Again. Closer.

She glanced out the side window. A man was coming up the path.

'Come on,' she snarled. 'Come on.' She gunned the motor again.

'Need any help there?' called the man. She could see

him in the mirror. He was shielding his face against the light.

Maybe he hadn't seen her. Maybe it would be OK. 'Come on. Come *on*.' She was almost weeping with rage. With fear. If he'd seen her face . . .

'Can I do anything?' he said from right beside her. She turned and looked him full in the face. He was quite old, about her dad's age, she thought vaguely. 'What's this then, rally trials?' he asked. Who did he think he was, Jack Dee? she thought. Bloody comedian had seen her now. She pumped the pedal again. 'How did you end up this far down, anyway?' She couldn't answer him. Couldn't the stupid bastard see what he was going to make her do? She didn't want to hurt him, but he wasn't leaving her any choice. 'Calm down, calm down,' he said. He touched her on the arm. Touched her! Patronising pig, she thought. It calmed her down. She knew what she had to do now. 'Let's have a bash,' he said. He reached inside and grabbed the wheel.

She pumped the accelerator, and this time the car leapt forward. The man was thrown to the side. He reeled away, then got his balance.

'Dozy cow, you could've taken me bloody arm off!' he screamed. He was standing right behind the van. Janice craned round to look at him out of the driver's window. Too stupid to live, she thought. She hadn't wanted to hurt him. She wasn't a cold-blooded murderer. There were just some things she had to do.

The dog yipped at something it had found. The man looked away. 'Here, boy,' he called.

Janice put the van into reverse. She floored the accelerator and the van hurtled towards the man. He looked round just in time to see her coming. The stupid bastard realised what was happening just in time to look frightened.

She watched as the van crunched into him. She had to be sure. The body fell back down the slope as the van coasted to a halt.

She squeezed her eyes shut. In the distance the damn dog was still barking. She wished there had been another way. He was an old man, not like the others. He wasn't part of her plan. But he'd been arrogant, just like the others. There really wasn't that much difference.

Should have got the damn dog as well, she thought, as she accelerated away.

'There, that wasn't so bad, was it?'

Jane Penhaligon smiled at Alan Temple. 'No,' she said. 'Not bad at all.'

She put her key in the front door.

'I'll see you tomorrow, then?' he said. He smiled. Nice smile, Penhaligon thought, as she had before. It didn't make him seem any less tense, though.

Penhaligon pushed the door open. 'First thing,' she said, knowing he wanted to kiss her goodnight. The thought set her pulse racing, but for all the wrong reasons. Don't touch me, she thought at him. Please.

He still didn't move. 'I'll be off, then.'

Penhaligon smiled at him. 'Drive safe,' she said. At last he turned and headed towards the outer door. Just before he got there, she said, 'Alan?' He turned. 'Thanks,' she said. 'It was a nice night out.'

'Glad you enjoyed it,' he answered. 'Do it again sometime?'

116

'I'd like that,' she said, and was surprised to realise she meant it.

'Good.' He smiled, and this time there was no tension in it. He pulled open the door and went through.

Penhaligon went into her flat. She let the door slam shut behind her, then leaned against it.

Just a date, that's all, she thought. She was trembling.

The phone began to ring.

They never seemed to find dead bodies in the middle of the day, Judith thought as she watched Fitz hurry down towards the police car that was waiting for him in their driveway. James grizzled at her shoulder. She patted his back absently.

That was Penhaligon in the driver's seat of the car. Stick insect, as she'd taken to calling her. The enemy by any name.

Detective Inspector Wise came up to Fitz. He was scowling. Of course, Judith remembered, his wife had left him after Fitz had counselled her. Well, he seemed to have put all that aside. He handed Fitz a letter.

'We intercepted it at the sorting office,' she heard him say. 'She says there's another body – a John Branaghan.'

'She?' Fitz asked.

'Got the results back from Forensics,' Wise said. 'There are smudges where she was holding the paper, like she was wearing gloves. They're too small to be a man's, so we go with her being a woman.'

'And this Branaghan's a student at Queen's?' Fitz asked. It meant nothing to Judith, and she wondered if she should go inside now. The night air was cold and damp, and she didn't want James catching a chill. But she had to see what happened when he got into the car with Penhaligon. Whether they smiled at each other. Gave any sign that they'd been together earlier ... anything that would tell her Fitz had been lying.

He got to the car just before Wise, and got in the back. Wise got in the front, and only then did Penhaligon acknowledge their presence.

Judith found she was smiling. It was a victory of a sort, she supposed.

Wise, closely followed by Fitz, edged his way through the trees down the steep incline to where the first body had been found. The second was closer to the top of the slope, near a patch of churned-up mud and grass.

He glanced round the scene, making sure he knew what was going on and what procedures were being followed. The area had been taped off and a couple of uniforms were standing by in case anyone should happen by. Several squad cars – marked and unmarked – were slewed across the road, and the glare of their headlights provided enough illumination for everyone to work by.

There was a woman sitting in the back of one of the squad cars. As he watched, a WPC in a fluorescent yellow waterproof handed her a cup of something. God knows where she'd found it, but he wished she'd get one for him.

Still at least the lads were right on top of things – a couple of SOCOs were already scouring the muddy earth for clues, and Skelton was giving directions to a pair of photographers. Good lad, Skelton, Wise thought approvingly. Showed initiative. He'd go far if he kept his nose clean.

Temple came up to meet Wise. 'It's him,' he said. 'John Branaghan.' He handed Wise a student union card. The victim laughed at him out of the photo. Well, you aren't laughing now, are you sunshine, Wise thought. Temple gestured at the body. 'Identical MO,' he said.

The corpse lay head first down the incline. It was partly in a pool of water, and there was a sack partially covering the chalk-white body.

Wise handed the card to Fitz, who stared at it for a moment. He glanced at the body. 'Pure bloody waste,' he said.

The other body was up the slope – a man in late middle age, fully clothed. Blood was seeping through his jacket. It couldn't be coincidence, Wise thought. Most likely the poor bugger had interrupted the killer as she dumped the body. Not that he wanted to jump to conclusions.

He turned back to Temple. 'You were fast?' he said.

Temple pointed to the squad car where the woman was sitting. 'Her husband took the dog for a walk. Couple of hours and he hadn't come home, she phoned the locals,' he said. 'The dog led 'em down there. Massive impact injuries – he only died a couple of minutes ago.' He turned and gestured at the second body. 'Judging by the tyre tracks, he got hit by a car. I assume we connect them?'

'Well it's not the M62 is it?' Wise said.

He looked again at the second body. He isn't that

119

much older than me, he thought. His wife was over in the car, sobbing her bloody heart out. He wondered if Rene would have cried like that if he'd been the one down there.

He doubted it.

Fitz stared round at the crowd in the incident room over the top of his half-moon reading glasses. The pale light of the overhead projector leached colour from their faces and made them seem even more tired than they surely must be.

Panhandle sipped from a can of shandy. She was sitting right up close to Temple. The sight of them together like that etched itself on to his brain. Right up close. Touching close.

He forced himself to think about the letter instead. Every word, every nuance, every possible ounce of meaning and implication. He placed it flat on the projection glass, and suddenly there it was up for all the world to see – someone protesting absolute undying love for him: which was rubbish of course, because what she was protesting wasn't love, it wasn't even infatuation. It was obsession, love turned in on itself and become like acid, burning away all true emotion, all real need, all honest caring.

But that was a lecture for another day.

' "The man who came to dinner tonight brought me chocolates," ' he read. ' "He thinks that's all there is to it, but you and me both know it takes much more than that to make someone love you." ' He paused. '*Dinner*. Coming to dinner. Middle-class concept.' He looked round at them, making sure they were following. He

120

tapped the letter and continued. 'But here she says "you and me both know", not "you and I" so her education's flawed.' He hesitated, working that one through in his mind. 'Upper working-class background with aspirations. Small-business family.' There was more, stuff one of them ought to have thought of, but it was worth saying just in case. 'She doesn't share a flat because she's frying these guys in private. Shifting the bodies without being seen, so she has access to money.' At least they were paying attention. The days when he had to prove his worth to them were long gone. He went back to the letter. He wasn't watching Panhandle at all. ' "Brought me chocolates" – who tries to charm a student with chocolates? A bottle of cider possibly. But they don't use foreplay – it's a well-known fact.' At least, it had been a well-known fact when he'd been one, and he couldn't see things changing that radically. 'Unless she was older than the victims. Unless John Branaghan took chocolates to a mature student, a late learner who resents the men she's sleeping with. Enough so as to want to execute them.'

That was it, he was sure. He looked round the room triumphantly. At Panhandle, hoping for a smile of encouragement.

Nothing.

'That it, then?' Wise asked. He came to the front of the room. 'Identical tyre tracks at all three murders,' he said, pacing.

'The third was incidental,' Fitz corrected. 'She only killed him because he'd seen her face.' Wise looked daggers at him. 'Separate motive,' Fitz explained. He didn't want Wise thinking he was being bolshie. Not given the man's current opinion of him.

'Identical tracks at all *three* murders,' Wise repeated. 'It's the only clue we've got. We go over every motor registered to the student car park first thing.'

He went over to the overhead projector and swapped the letter for a street map of the area. 'Now,' he said, 'she posted the first letter here, very close to the body, the last letter at 11.30 tonight.' He checked his watch. '*Last* night, at the sorting office, here. If she travels south to the university, she passes both these every day. Familiar route. So she lives somewhere in there.'

Fitz thought that was just too pat – she'd been smart so far. There was no reason to expect she lived near where she'd dumped the bodies. He didn't say anything, though. If he were going to burn the carpet – if he were going to make a concerted effort to save his marriage – then he had to let Judith see he was bringing money into the house. And not spending it faster than he could make it, but that was a separate issue.

'Just as a thought,' he said, 'we know she shackled her victims – metal shackles on both wrists and one ankle. The other one had rope burns. So where'd she get them?'

'Sex shops?' Panhandle asked. She wasn't smiling. Not quite.

'But why the rope?' Temple asked. He *was* smiling.

'I don't know,' she said. 'Maybe they sold out of ankle cuffs?' And now she was grinning too. Laughter rattled round the room.

Fitz scowled. He knew what he was seeing. The only question in his mind was whether they saw it as well.

'All right, all right,' Wise said. 'Temple, tomorrow

you start checking sex shops. Take a couple of people with you, all right?'

Panhandle turned to Wise. 'Don't you think Fitz is a problem on this one, sir?'

Fitz stared at her. She looked back at him levelly. He heard her say again, *I don't love you, Fitz*. Maybe she didn't. Maybe she believed she didn't. But he hadn't thought she found him that difficult to be around.

'What's special about this one?' Temple asked, just as if they'd been rehearsing it.

'If she's writing him love letters, he's a target and we have to address his influence on the case.' Panhandle sipped her shandy.

She might have had a point, if she'd analysed the situation correctly. But she hasn't, Fitz thought. She can't have, because if she has then I'm out and I can't be out – because of Judith. Because of Panhandle. 'She isn't looking for love, she wants understanding,' he said, and knew he was blustering.

'From you?' Panhandle challenged.

'From the world.'

'But she's writing to *you*,' Panhandle insisted. It was that sheer bloody-mindedness that Fitz loved, and that Beck had hated. The determination that had seen her through the dark days after the rape and the loss of Giggs and Bilborough to serial killers. 'She says she loves you.'

'People do,' he said, daring her to say openly that she didn't believe that was possible.

Temple took Panhandle's can without asking. He sipped from it then put it back in her hand. They are . . . Fitz thought. But before he could decide just what they were doing, Temple said, 'But I agree with Jane.'

Jane! Fitz thought. He'd only ever called her that in bed. It was too intimate for everyday. He looked at them, at their closeness, the way their body language pointed inwards at each other.

And he knew.

The knowledge made him furious. Blind rage, coming up from nowhere. He'd thought he was sorry to lose her. He was wrong. He was ready to kill to keep her.

'If she's writing to you and she's displacing her love, need for understanding,' Temple said, 'whatever you want to call it –'

'Displacement, is it?' Fitz snarled. 'We've had one sausage roll in the psychology department canteen and suddenly we're Sigmund Freud, are we?' He turned on Panhandle. 'You said that without moving your lips.' She glared at him.

'She's still writing to you,' Temple said calmly.

'No she's writing to *you*,' Fitz shouted. 'She's writing to the police because she wants to be caught, you dumb bastard.'

'Ay ay,' Wise said.

Fitz took a long, deep breath. Kill to keep Panhandle? There was a concept their mystery killer would understand.

'You're missing the point, Fitz,' she said, just as if she wanted to wind him up.

'*Am* I?'

'The letters are for you. The bodies are for you.' He stared at her. Her eyes were dark shadows in the milky whiteness of her face. He thought she'd never seemed more beautiful than now, when he'd lost her for

124

sure. 'She's trying to make you jealous,' Panhandle explained. 'She's killed three people for *you*.'

He stared at her, knowing she was right. It wasn't his fault, but they were dead. Not because of him, but for him, because of his failure to love someone.

She wanted him to feel guilty. To take the blame. He stared at Panhandle and saw it written in her face.

And he knew then what she must have felt all along, even if she wouldn't admit it: that when Beck raped her, it was somehow because he, Fitz, hadn't loved her enough. Hadn't protected her.

Maybe, he thought, maybe it's even true.

NINE

Janice pulled her van over to join the line of cars waiting to go into the university car park. She climbed out to see what the problem was. Squinting into the sun, she saw a couple of coppers checking the tyres of vehicles as they entered.

Well that's bloody stupid of them, she thought. As if she'd drive straight into the trap, when she knew she must have left tracks.

It was an insult, she decided as she got back into the van. They obviously thought she was stupid. Well, she'd show them. She was in far too good a mood after last night to let a minor setback like this get on top of her.

Grinning to herself, she turned the van round, checking carefully to make sure she hadn't been seen.

What they didn't understand, she thought as she drove to the garage, was that getting caught because of a stupid mistake wasn't part of the story.

No, there was only one possible happy ending – the one where Fitz realised he loved her, had loved her all along, and they both lived happily ever after. But first he had to notice her, and how could he with some clodhopping policemen getting in the way?

She drove past the first few garages she saw. It might

just occur to them to check, Fitz might even suggest it himself. The thought made her smile. Finally, she found one that was far enough away from the university for safety.

She got out and told the garage hand what she wanted. There were a couple of other cars waiting to be seen to, and a couple more with FOR SALE signs on them. Briefly, she considered trading the van in for one. But a car wouldn't suit her needs half so well, and besides she couldn't really afford it.

The garage hand kicked her tyres. 'You sure, love? These have got plenty of tread on 'em,' he said.

Janice lit up a cigarette. 'Yeah, well you tell that to the copper who pulled me over last night,' she said. She took a drag. 'Look, I'm in a bit of a hurry –'

'Yeah, yeah,' he answered. He called to one of his mates and they jacked the van up.

Janice stood off to one side and smoked as she watched them work. Had she left any other clues? She couldn't think of any – not fingerprints, and, from what he'd said, Branaghan hadn't told his mates where he was going. Why would he? Dowdy little Janice the lab technician was hardly a lay to boast about. She crossed one arm in front of her. If one of them, just one of them, had thought differently, maybe she wouldn't have had to . . . but she just wasn't going to think about that. About what might have been if things at home had been more normal. If she'd been prettier. Or brighter. Or –

She felt her eyes start to prickle with tears. Much more of that and they'd be asking if she were all right, and that would mean that afterwards they'd remember

128

who she was. She couldn't have that. She looked round carefully at the garage, at the sunlight striking rainbows off the oily water on the forecourt, at the middle-aged couple earnestly considering the merits of the second-hand Volvo against those of the Renault next to it.

'You want the carwash, love?' the garage hand asked. 'There's a special offer this week –'

'No,' she said, shortly.

'Suit yourself,' he answered. He wasn't bad looking, Janice thought. If she'd been Louise, she'd have had him drooling after her. He'd have given her the damn carwash for free. Not that she wanted it. She didn't want the police thinking she'd cleaned the van up specially – that, for instance, she'd cleaned splashes of mud off the wheel arches.

'Look, I'm in a hurry, all right?' she said, and cursed herself for thinking she had to explain herself to him.

'All right, all right, love.' He told her how much the tyres were, and she paid him.

There was still a bit of a queue when she got back to the university. This time she took her turn at the checkpoint, behind a beaten-up Sierra.

One of the coppers came over to her, clutching a clipboard. He leaned in at the window. He was rather interesting, she thought, with beautiful dark eyes and a smile that lit up his face. If her mind hadn't been on other things, she might have found him quite attractive.

'Mind if we check your tyres, madam?' he asked. 'Only take a sec.'

'Check what you like,' Janice answered, making sure she met his gaze. That's what Louise said, look 'em in

129

the eye. Dare them to guess what you're thinking. Sure enough, he hesitated for a moment before he bent to check her tyres.

I know what you're thinking, she thought at him. Dirty-minded little bastard.

He stood up and wrote something down.

'All right?' Janice asked.

'In you go, love,' he said. He scarcely looked at her.

She drove into the car park. Her good mood had vanished, and she felt miserable. That copper had scarcely had a civil word for her, once he'd got what he wanted. And as for Fitz, well for all she knew they hadn't even found the body yet. She scowled and started the long trek through the psychology department to Irene Jackson's office. Down the corridor, round the corner, up the stairs and along the top corridor . . . he probably didn't even know anything had happened last night, let alone that it was all for him.

She rounded the final corner and started towards her room. Music. Her music. That minor key was unmistakable. *It isn't the way that you look, And it isn't the way that you talk* . . . she hesitated outside the door. They were playing her music. The gall of them. But she'd have to go in. Too many people had seen her. *It's the way you make me feel, Whenever I am close to you* . . . She opened the door and went in.

Irene Jackson was standing by the window, next to the portable hi-fi she used to blast the place with the Bach she swore she needed to work by. Sunlight streamed in. It was a glorious day, but you'd never have guessed it from the scowl on her face.

'Afternoon,' Irene said tartly, though in fact it wasn't

yet ten thirty. To Janice's relief she clicked the cassette recorder off.

'I thought you were out all day,' Janice replied, stung. You took half an hour off to see to important personal business and you'd think she'd swanned off for a month.

Irene put the cassette into a file marked *Fitz*. 'There's been another murder.'

The words hung heavy in the bright air. Janice had to restrain herself from smiling. 'Oh my God,' she said, pouring sincerity into her words. 'It's getting so's you daren't go out.' That should do it, she thought. But then she realised she'd better ask the obvious question. She went over to the kettle, and as she plugged it in she said, 'Who?'

'John Branaghan,' Irene said. She seemed truly upset. Janice refrained from asking her if she meant the arrogant little Jack the Lad in the second year, though that had been one of the reasons she'd chosen him. 'We've all been summoned to the Lecture Theatre,' Irene went on.

Irene picked her bag up and slung it over her shoulder. She picked Fitz's notes up off the table, then headed towards the door. 'I know we're busy but I might be out a lot. Dr Leishman's going to be standing in for me.'

Janice turned to her. 'Anything you want me to do?' she asked.

Irene paused. 'How many mature students this year?'

Mature students, Janice thought, outraged. First he gave her tape to Irene to play, then he went completely off the track. Mature bloody students! 'About thirty-five,' she said after the merest pause. That was OK,

131

though. Irene was no Fitz. She was more at home with her statistical models of rats' learning behaviour than she was with people. She'd just think Janice was trying to remember.

'Women?'

Janice blinked, just once but slowly. If Irene was half what she was supposed to be, she couldn't have missed that, Janice thought. But the stupid woman obviously hadn't been listening to anything Fitz said about passion and commitment and the way psychology had to link to real people or be nothing worth studying.

'I can check.'

Again, Irene let it pass. 'See you down there.' She went out. The door clicked shut behind her.

That stupid, stupid woman, Janice thought. The rage was a red tide within her. Irene bloody Jackson was so close to Fitz and she never listened to him and Janice wanted him so much and he hadn't even noticed she was there and John Branaghan had pleaded and Steven Lowry had begged and she hadn't listened and Fitz wasn't listening to her. The tide rose up and would have engulfed her with waves of incandescent rage. It had to find a way out. She raised her hand, meaning to sweep the kettle off the shelf. Her muscles tensed. But someone would hear. They'd find her out before she was ready, before she'd forced Fitz to listen to her, to love her. Slowly, she lowered her hand. She breathed out, long and hard. And in. She would be calm. Gently, she turned the kettle on.

Penhaligon didn't know which scared her most, the assembled throng of psychology students in the main

132

lecture hall, or the hard eyes of the staff. They all seemed to have expected miracles, if not an arrest, at least judging by the comments they'd made before the meeting.

Well, she'd faced even worse. At least this time she hadn't had to face grieving parents.

She stared round at the students. Two buckets were making the rounds, collections for Branaghan and Lowry. 'Nobody's asking you to stop dating,' she said, turning her head to make sure she kept everyone's attention. 'But if you *are* making arrangements for a new relationship, we're asking everybody – *not* just people in the psychology department –' God, she thought, I sound just like the worst kind of teacher '– to tell *somebody* where they're going –'

'But only if you're expecting sex,' one of the male students said, grinning slyly. He was wearing a tee-shirt that looked like it might have been clean around the time the dinosaurs became extinct, and judging by the way he bulged out of it he'd been living on pizza and greaseburgers.

'No,' Penhaligon said.

The collection bucket came to the student. He handed it on without really looking at it. Light flashed on his wire-rimmed spectacles. He leered at her, and turned round to make sure his mates were listening. 'But you're putting it on record that group sex is definitely safer, then?'

That won him a smattering of laughter.

Smartarse, Penhaligon thought. 'Depends what condition you're in,' she snapped. That got a lot more laughter than the student had. He had the good grace to look uncomfortable.

'You've skipped the collection, by the way,' an older woman student called from behind him. He hesitated then pulled a few coins out of his pocket, leaned over and threw them into the bucket, which was now a few people away from him.

God, Penhaligon thought, she could be the one. If Fitz is right, she could be. She's even blonde, like that hair we found.

The Vice-Chancellor stepped up on the dais next to her, interrupting her train of thought. 'Thank you, Detective Sergeant Penhaligon,' he said. She smiled and moved towards the door, where, she now realised, Fitz was waiting. He was puffing on a cigarette in open defiance of the NO SMOKING sign above his head. She smiled at him, knowing he thought she'd betrayed him, but not even being able to summon enough energy to care, let alone put it right. If it were worth putting right.

The Vice-Chancellor turned to the students. 'Thank you for your co-operation,' he said. 'For Group A this morning's schedule will continue as planned with . . .' he looked round. Fitz dropped his dog-end on the floor and stubbed it out with his toe, then sauntered forward. He hadn't once acknowledged Penhaligon's presence. '. . . Doctor Fitzgerald.'

About half the students got up. There was a moment of confusion as they pushed past those remaining, who took the opportunity to chat. There was little laughter.

Fitz glared round at the students, waiting for the buzz of conversation to end and the last stragglers to leave. Penhaligon could see him assessing them, deciding who, in his opinion, was likely to break. Who might be a suspect.

He sniffed. 'OK, let's talk about human nature.' He paused. 'Here's a joke for you.' He had their attention now. It wasn't a time for joking, and they all knew it. 'I found it on the wall in the engineering block toilets,' he said. ' "How many psychology students does it take to change a fuse?" ' A few people shifted uncomfortably. ' "Two so far," ' Fitz said. The audience sucked in its collective breath. Penhaligon stared at Fitz, wondering how she'd ever been in love with him, with that capacity for inflicting discomfort. 'Does anybody find that funny?' Fitz demanded. He stepped down from the dais and started to pace back and forth in front of the students as he spoke. 'Come on,' he said. He caught the eye of one of the mature students. She looked away quickly. 'I laughed,' he said. Well you would, Penhaligon thought. 'It's sick, witty, savage – good going for an engineer.' That was just typical Fitz, in Penhaligon's view – never a compliment without a putdown coming right behind it.

Fitz turned and went back on to the dais. 'It's all of that – but it's denial. Denial of the death that's coming for us all. It's a way of laughing in the face of the darkness. But it's also denial of the life, of the light that makes it impossible for us all to ignore our flaws.' He turned to Penhaligon. 'We all have them, you know, even me.' That got a laugh, and the atmosphere lightened. But Fitz scowled at her as if to add, *even you*. All right, she thought, if that's the way you want to play it. Before he looked away she headed outside. The heavy glass door swung slowly open, and the cooler air of the hall hit her. Behind her, she heard Fitz say, 'Without denial, half of you would have to face the *truth* that you're too ugly, too fat, too thin, too sensitive, too passive, too angry to survive this world.' She paused to listen. She couldn't help herself: when she looked at him, she could remember she no longer loved him; but his voice, with its heavy Scottish accent and its hint of smoker's throat, always held her. 'There'd be carnage,' he said. 'Suicides. At the moment, we're only looking at two murdered students. So don't knock denial.'

Denial, Penhaligon mused as she started down the corridor. Her feet rang on the tiled floor. The question was, had she been denying something when she thought she was in love with Fitz? Or was she denying something now, when she was sure she wasn't?

She shoved her hands in her jacket pockets and walked away from the sound of his voice.

TEN

Fitz dragged on his cigarette, then exhaled. A cloud of blue smoke almost obscured Wise's shocked face.

Fitz leaned across the table. He spoke urgently, but not so loudly that any of the other students in the Union bar would overhear. 'Come on, this is your cast-iron, once-in-a-lifetime wish fulfilment,' he said. Wise's trouble was, he never knew when he was well off. 'You fire me –'

'You what?' Wise said, though Fitz had already made the suggestion once.

'Public humiliation,' Fitz elaborated. 'Tell 'em what a useless tosser I turned out to be.' He sighed. He hated having to admit he was wrong even more than he hated the idea of going home and telling Judith that he'd once again lost the job. But it had to be done. Truth had to be served. And if possible they had to stop the killings. 'Penhaligon was right. She's writing to me, she's killing for me.' Wise glared at him as if he were the man's best friend and he'd just stabbed him in the back, rather than the man he blamed for the breakdown of his marriage. 'Take me off the case,' Fitz insisted.

Wise was shocked. 'Where does that leave us?'

Working it out for yourselves, doing what Jimmy bloody Beck would doubtless have called good old-fashioned coppering, Fitz thought. He stubbed his fag-end out in the ashtray with fingers like nicotine-stained sausages. The only trouble was, given the general competence of Wise's bunch of half-trained monkeys, three quarters of the student body would be dead before they got within ten miles of the killer.

Then he twisted round on his seat. Irene was at the bar. He caught her attention, and she brought her whisky over to them.

She took the seat between Fitz and Wise. 'You two've met,' Fitz said. 'I've given Irene the case details. I trust her judgement, OK?' Irene smiled. She seemed nervous, which was something Fitz had rarely seen. Wise nodded to her. He wasn't smiling. 'You make a press release stating categorically that Irene's been installed.'

'You think that'll stop the killing?' Wise asked Irene.

'I've no idea,' she answered. Wrong answer, Fitz thought. He knew she was uncomfortable with the idea of police work. She was more of an academic. If she could pin something down to numbers, she was happy. If she could model it mathematically, she was happier still. It hurt Fitz to admit it, but she'd make exactly the kind of police psychologist Fitz most despised – one who'd give Wise a percentage of probability of what the killer ate for breakfast, and no insight whatsoever into her screwed-up little brain. Now she said tentatively, 'If Fitz is her focus and he's removed, it could drive her out into the open.' She fiddled with one of the pins in her long greying hair. 'She's organised both murders very precisely.'

'Three,' Wise said firmly.

Irene looked startled. She turned to Fitz. 'I thought the third was incidental?' She had a lot to learn about the police mind. Fitz was only worried she wouldn't learn it fast enough.

'Tell his wife that,' Wise said before Fitz could react. He swigged his beer, obviously hoping to forestall further conversation.

Fitz leaned forward in his seat. He looked Wise straight in the eye and said, 'We need her to make a few mistakes before she nails some other poor bastard.'

Over Wise's shoulder, Skelton came into the bar. He stood at the door for a moment, then spotted them. 'Sir,' he called.

Wise turned round, Skelton hurried over. He bent close to Wise's ear, and said in an undertone, 'Sorry, sir. They've intercepted another letter.'

Wise pushed himself to his feet. 'Excuse me,' he said. He started out of the bar without waiting for the others.

Fitz got up to follow him, then remembered Irene. 'Coming?' he asked.

'No,' she said. 'No. I need time to think about this. I'll talk to you later.'

Fitz left. He didn't let himself scowl till he was facing away from her. Some other poor sod was going to die, and she was too scared to do anything about it.

Well, he supposed he shouldn't have expected anything more from a psychologist who preferred to stay in her nice clean laboratory rather than get out and face the dark heart of humanity.

Even if she did play a mean game of poker.

The sound of Wise and Fitz coming down the hall was

unmistakable – Wise heavy but rapid, Fitz even heavier but slower.

Penhaligon smiled slightly at Temple, who was checking through statements taken from friends of Lowry and Branaghan. Neither of them were wholly comfortable when Fitz was around. He smiled back. She picked up her photocopy of the newest letter and leaned against a filing cabinet facing the door, so that by the time they came in she was ready for them.

She went forward to meet Wise. Fitz followed him in with Skelton bringing up the rear. She said, 'We've compared it with the three lecture transcripts,' she said, showing Wise the photocopy. He nodded approvingly. 'She says here, "you talk about devotion. I've never been more devoted in my life". That was the –'

'Second lecture,' Fitz said, so they were speaking together. She glanced up at him. He looked straight at her, and for a moment it was just like old times, Fitz and Panhandle running rings round Jimmy Beck. But I don't want that, she thought sadly.

Fitz started to read. ' "The man I've got coming to dinner tonight ..." ' he said. He looked at her, apparently trying to see if she'd picked up on whatever he thought he'd found. 'Future tense – that's new. She's always sent the letters after she killed them.'

'And she's always given us a name,' Penhaligon added, just to let him know she'd been paying attention.

Wise turned to Temple. 'Get on to the university. Names and addresses of all mature students listed for the second lecture.'

Temple picked up the phone. 'For a woman who wants to be caught she's not offering much.'

140

Such a nice voice, Penhaligon thought. Not that she was thinking about him like that. She'd fallen into that trap once. She wasn't going to do it twice. She started going through her notes. And I'm not – I am not – falling in love. Yet she couldn't resist a quick glance in Temple's direction – only to find Fitz staring at her.

He scowled and turned away, then lunged past Temple. He grabbed the forensic bag that contained the envelope the letter had come in.

'But more than you deserve, Noddy,' he snarled.

Oh grow up, Penhaligon thought.

Fitz shoved the bag at Temple. 'Is this what it came in?'

'Why?' Temple snapped back, obviously not getting it.

But then he hardly ever seemed to. Penhaligon did wonder a bit how he'd ever made it to DI, when she couldn't.

'There's no stamp on it – she's telling us she knows we're intercepting her mail.'

Temple stared at him. Just for one second all Penhaligon could think was, he got busted. All the way from Inspector to Constable. The reason didn't matter, not with Fitz having to spell out everything for him like that.

'She wouldn't forget to put the stamp on it.' Temple just stared at him. 'She's showing me how bright she is,' Fitz explained.

Temple still didn't get it. 'So?'

Fitz took a long, deep breath. He paced slowly across the room, so he could look at all of them. When he spoke again, his tone was full of exaggerated patience.

'If she knows you've got it already, "tonight" means *tonight*, not tomorrow.' He was looking round at all of them. She saw everyone's expression slowly registering what Fitz had already worked out. 'She's going to kill again *tonight*, for God's sake.'

ELEVEN

Concentration wasn't Frank Weetman's strong suit.

Just at the moment, he couldn't concentrate at all. He was sitting on the sofa in Janice's flat. Janice was right next to him. She was wearing a black dress so tight it should have been illegal, and her perfume – musk and roses – hung heavy on the air. She wasn't quite touching him, but she didn't need to – he could imagine it all too well himself.

That was the trouble, of course. He was supposed to be talking about the essay. Steven's essay. His essay, as it now was. 'I think what I was trying to achieve in that . . .' but it was no good. He kept noticing the curve of her breast under the thin cloth of her dress. 'In that statement was a kind of . . .' It was ridiculous. She had her hair up, and she was wearing one of those things round her neck. A choker. With a pearl in it. He didn't know any girls who dressed like that. She was obviously way out of his class. He shifted in the sofa, but now his leg was touching hers. Quickly, he moved it back. 'Some kind of general overview . . .' he said, desperately. If he touched her now . . . if he made a move . . . but it was just stupid. She'd slap his face, have him out the flat in one second flat. And yet, she hadn't moved her leg away. He'd moved his. So would she think he wasn't interested? God, how could anybody not be interested in her?

'You're not concentrating, are you, Frank?' she said. Her voice was low and sexy, and he didn't know if she was teasing or what.

'Sorry,' he said, far too quickly. If she knew what he'd been thinking about –

'Go on then,' she said.

'What?'

'Touch me,' she said.

Bloody hell, he thought. He shifted again on the seat and felt his leg touch hers, his erection rub against his pants.

'It's what you want,' she said. 'It's what you came for.'

He shook his head. He couldn't do this. He wanted it, but he couldn't do it. He was never any good at this kind of thing and –

She leaned over and put her hand on his crotch. 'Liar,' she said.

He hadn't thought he could get any harder, but he did now.

She was watching him with those eyes he could drown in, and yet he still didn't dare move. His throat was dry. If he wasn't any good . . . she moved towards him, and smiled slightly. And then there was nothing he could do but lean in and kiss those honey-filled lips, and nothing in the world that could have stopped him.

She wasn't going to turn up. Danny Fitzgerald was sure of it. He stared around at the restaurant, at the gold dragons and red pillars. At the couples sharing intimate moments at other tables, while he sat alone, trying not to check his watch every thirty seconds. He'd read somewhere that the Chinese believe both dragons and the colour red are lucky.

It seemed they were wrong.

He realised he was tapping his fingers on the tablecloth, and forced himself to stop.

A waiter walked past him. Danny turned, and saw Judith coming down the stairs. She hesitated for a moment, searching for him. She was wearing a sapphire-blue dress that intensified the red lights in her hair. She looked wonderful. Danny realised suddenly that he was literally breathless with desire.

Danny stood up. She saw him and came over. She smiled. Was that nervousness or shyness? Danny wondered, and realised how little he really knew her. He gestured for her to sit down, then helped her. As he bent close to push her chair in, he smelled the apple scent of her shampoo. The dress was silky, like her skin. If he'd wanted to, he could have touched it . . . And what, he wondered, would she have done then?

Eddie would have known. But Danny wasn't Eddie, and he was glad of it. He'd settle for learning people slowly. And not hurting them.

But he couldn't let the moment pass entirely. 'Nice dress,' he whispered.

A nice blue dress, he thought, and went to take his own seat. A nice *blue* dress.

'Well, you paid for it,' Judith said.

'Oh, come on.' There was nowhere for him to look but at her, and that dress. Buy something blue, he'd said. And she had. But had she bought it because he said to, or for him, because she thought he'd like her in it?

'Which is why I'm paying for the meal,' Judith said. 'Don't argue.' The waiter came over. She turned to him. Her long earrings danced and flashed in the soft light. 'Gin and tonic, please. Danny?'

'Just ordered one,' he said.

She smiled at him. She seemed happier than she had since James was born. Danny only hoped she was going to stay that way.

Wise hammered at Maureen Kiernan's front door. Light glowed through the textured glass. A shadow moved in the hall beyond.

Maureen Kiernan, Wise supposed: thirty-three years old, second-year psychology student, like the two dead men. They'd had eleven possibles, whittled those down to five either because of where they lived or because their grant status showed they were married. The rest had blown out, one way or another.

The door opened. Maureen Kiernan glared out at them. 'Yeah?' she demanded. She looked every minute of thirty-three: a plain, angular woman with dirty blonde hair. If anyone was going to match the profile Fitz and Forensics had come up with, it was her.

Wise shoved his warrant card in her face. 'Mind if we come in, love?' he said, and barged past her. Penhaligon, Temple and Skelton followed her in.

'Hey!' she shouted 'Hey!!'

They ignored her and piled into the front room. Temple radioed the station to let them know what was going on, while Penhaligon and Skelton raced upstairs.

'What the bloody hell's going on?' Kiernan demanded.

There were books and papers scattered all over the front-room table. Wise started rooting through them. Fitz had said she might have taken photos. 'You're a student at Queen's aren't you?' If she wasn't, she should have been – some of the books on the table must have been two inches thick.

'Have you a key for the back door, love?' Temple called. He'd gone through into the open-plan kitchen. 'Are there any –' A baby started to wail, cutting through what Temple was saying. He raised his voice. '– out-buildings?'

The song from the tape, Wise thought. She must have copied it from somewhere. He looked around for a hi-fi system.

'I'll bloody murder you,' Kiernan screamed. 'It's taken me two hours to get them to sleep.' She grabbed the books Wise was holding. 'You get them down here now or I'm calling a solicitor.'

Wise spotted the hi-fi, and went over to it. For a minute he thought Kiernan might thump him one, but she turned away and grabbed the phone and started punching out a number.

Temple came up beside her. 'Have you a key, love?' he asked.

Kiernan stopped dialling. 'You call me love once more and I'll smack you right in the bloody mouth,' she snarled.

Penhaligon and Skelton came downstairs. 'Nothing, boss,' Penhaligon said.

'What the bloody hell do you mean, *nothing*?' Kiernan demanded.

'Means we're sorry to have bothered you,' Wise said, and added the 'love' before he could stop himself. 'You lot, back to the station. Looks like Fitz has won again.'

But then, Wise thought, he always bloody did.

'You've never met such a vindictive lot of proprietorial bastards in all your life,' Judith said. Danny smiled, which made his eyes crinkle up. She fiddled with her fingers, trying not to look at him. He's actually interested, Judith thought. He actually does care about what happens to me, about my job . . . about me . . . 'Why?' she said, and suddenly she had to touch him. She laid her hand gently on top of his. Her rings – eternity ring, engagement ring, wedding ring – glinted in the soft light. I shouldn't be doing this, she thought. Danny turned his hand over and began to stroke hers. 'Fear,' she said. They were holding hands now, across the table. 'Suddenly they're given salaries, cars . . .' but it was no use. She couldn't concentrate on anything but the gentle caress of his fingers. 'That feels so nice . . .' She was married. She'd made one mistake, when she'd slept with her therapist, Graham, but that was years ago. She wasn't going to make another. 'Salaries, cars, status,' she repeated. It was so much easier to talk about work than even to think about what she was feeling. Danny was watching her intently. She could almost feel his gaze, hot like the sun on her face. She took a deep breath. 'So they each have to prove they care more than anyone else, to justify the perks in the name of charity.' She smiled. 'Which is why they have to be managed by someone like me.' Danny was smiling too, now. 'Which is what I told them this morning. Which is why I've not only been given my job back, I've just been promoted.'

'Congratulations,' Danny said, but he only gave her the tiniest of smiles. 'My brother's been teaching you bad habits.' Now what the hell did he mean by that? Judith tried to snatch her hand away, but Danny grabbed it back. 'Judith, I take people seriously. I won't be messed about.'

Judith stared at him – at the crinkly, earnest eyes and the mouth that seemed to have forgotten how to smile – and for the first time she understood that this was real. That Danny's feelings were real. And so were her own.

Janice stared at shadows that danced by candlelight across the ceiling. Frank Weetman lay next to her. She could hear him breathing. At least he was better at that than he was at screwing. Well, what could you expect from a *boy*?

'I couldn't concentrate,' he said. He sounded defensive. Well so he bloody should, Janice thought. For all their faults, at least Steven Lowry and John Branaghan had given her a good time before –

Sure enough, Frank started to get out of bed. He searched around for his jeans. He had quite a nice back, Janice thought. Spotty, but nice.

'Aren't you stopping, then?' Janice asked. Stupid question. Why would he want to stay with *her*?

'No.'

So that was that, then. Janice rolled over, taking great care not to make a noise, and reached into the bedside drawer where she kept the cosh. No sex games for you, Frank Weetman, she thought. You don't deserve them.

'Would you want me to?' he asked.

The words went through Janice like a jolt of electricity. He wanted her. He wanted *her*. She slid the cosh back into the drawer and silently shut it.

'Would you?' he asked again.

She turned and stared at him. He swallowed. She reached for him in the flickering light, and for a time there was quiet.

Danny bent his head and, very gently, kissed the back of her fingers. The gold of her wedding ring was hard and cold. She's a married woman, said a small voice at the back of his brain. He ignored it.

'That feels so bloody wonderful ...' she said. Her eyes were a brown so dark they were almost black, and when she looked at him like that he would have done anything to please her. 'I feel just like a child.'

'But you're not a child, and I'm not Eddie,' he answered. His fingers were laced with hers now, twined inextricably just the way his feelings for her were. 'I have a longer attention span than my brother –'

'Twenty-six years is hardly hit and run,' she cut in.

How could he not love her, when she stood by Eddie despite the way he treated her? What would it be like, he wondered, to command such loyalty? Her skin was like silk beneath his fingers. If she wanted him – if she could love him, if she *would* – then, he resolved, he would earn her loyalty. 'When was the last time that he held you like this?' he asked, and the voice in his head said in outraged tones, she's your brother's *wife*.

'You're not just seeing this as a chance to get back at him?' she asked.

'No!' Danny stared at her, horrified at the very

notion. But there was a worse possibility. 'Are you?' The only answer she had for him was the confusion in her eyes. He bent his head close to her. 'You have to think very bloody carefully about what you're making me do, Judith.' He was forty-five years old. He'd never felt older or more afraid in his life.

She swallowed. For a moment he thought she wouldn't answer. Then she said, 'I am.'

TWELVE

There was an arm around her, pinning her to the bed. Panic surged through Janice before she remembered that Frank Weetman had stayed the night. She could hear him breathing, slow and regular, behind her. Her eyes flickered open. The grey light of early morning pearled through the gaps in the curtains.

That was right, she thought, he'd said the other room made him nervous. Maybe he was right. He'd certainly done a lot better once they came in here. She wriggled back, enjoying the feeling of his body against hers. If it could have been like this more often, she thought, if there could have been more just holding each other in the darkness and the quiet when all the world was asleep, maybe things could have been different. If she had found just one person who wanted to do that with her, maybe she wouldn't have had to try and take what she needed.

'Janice?' he whispered. 'You awake?' His voice was full of tenderness.

But it was too late for that, Janice realised. There was no way to go back, no way to stand still. All she could do was go forward and hope that she would come out into the clear bright light of Fitz's love at the end of it.

'Yeah,' she said.

His fingers moved across her breast. 'You want to . . .'

'No!' she said. 'Look, I'm sorry – you'd better go.' He'd been all right, second time around. Eager to please. Boyishly eager, in fact.

Well, she didn't want a boy.

He'd almost made her forget what she did want. She got up and wrapped her dressing gown round herself before he could get any ideas. Even so, he watched her as she went into the living room.

Let him. Let him do what he liked, she thought. She clicked the TV on, then lit a cigarette. The sound from the TV rolled over her. He wasn't cocky, like the others – no, he was just a loser.

'I'll be going then,' he said from behind her.

Janice turned round. He was fully dressed. 'See you around,' Janice said. He went and picked his essay up off the coffee table. 'It'll be fine – just needs a bit of tightening up,' Janice said, more to get rid of him than anything else.

'Yeah,' Frank said. His jaw worked. For an awful moment, Janice thought he was crying. 'Only it's not mine, is it? The one chance I'd got to stop myself being booted out . . . nicking a dead man's essay.' He looked at her, and sure enough tears glinted on his cheeks. 'And you go and pull it to pieces.'

Well, she knew how that felt all right. 'Just proves he wasn't all he cracked himself up to be,' she said. 'You shouldn't believe half of what that lot tell you, Frank. They don't know shit from sugar.'

'Yeah, well,' he said. He got as far as the door before

he said, 'Can I see you again?'

Janice stubbed her cigarette out. 'No. I've got some-one,' she said.

'Right.' He still didn't leave. He really was thick, she decided – not just the kind of thick that failed stupid college essays, but the kind of thick that didn't under-stand a bloody thing.

'Long-standing,' she explained. She wondered how to put it to him so he'd understand. She knew most people wouldn't. If it had been a rock star, people might have understood. But the one time she'd tried to explain it to her sisters, Nina had laughed in her face. So she'd just have to put it a way that he would understand. Maybe then he'd leave her alone. 'Well, we met five years back and it didn't work out. Both trying too hard, really, wanting it too much. We kept in touch, never stopped thinking about each other. But we're both older now and we've just realised how much time we've wasted.'

'So what was last night all about?' Frank demanded.

Christ, Janice thought. Now he thinks he owns me. 'You tell me,' she snarled. 'You, started it.'

His eyes went wide with shock, or perhaps hurt. She couldn't find it in her to care. 'Fine,' he said. 'If that's the way you want it.'

He still didn't go. 'It is,' Janice said. Any minute now the news would come on and she'd miss it because of this idiot. She glared at him.

He turned and left. The door slammed shut after him. Janice stared at the space where he had been, unable to quite put her finger on why she felt so lonely. No, she thought. Not lonely. Deflated, maybe, but that was simple to explain – it was because Frank Weetman was a poor substitute for Fitz.

She turned and switched the sound up on the TV. Just for a moment, it was as if she felt Frank's arms around her, holding her as he had that morning when she woke up. But that was ridiculous. She didn't want that. She wanted Fitz.

Accept no substitutes, she thought to herself wryly as the news cycled through the endless round of stories about Bosnia and the Royal Family and Northern Ireland.

Then the sport. She was sure she hadn't missed it. Her mouth pursed in irritation. So they didn't think what she'd done was worth talking about, was that it? She realised her fingers were clutching at the edge of her dressing gown. With an effort she made herself relax. She pulled out her cigarettes and lit up.

And then suddenly it was all right, because the local news came on, and there was Fitz's face staring out at her from behind the newsreader. Click – he was replaced by Steven Lowry. Click. John Branaghan. Maybe Fitz was going to talk about it, she thought. Maybe he'd praise the way she'd organised the crime. That was what he'd call her, she knew – an organised killer. He'd tell everyone that she'd been supremely careful in the way she'd arranged everything, so that the police had the fewest possible clues to work with. Maybe he'd even say that was because she wanted Fitz to solve the puzzle she set for him.

But Fitz didn't appear. The newsreader said, 'Anson Road police station has refused to issue detailed reasons for the psychologist's removal from the case –' *What?*

The word was a scream in Janice's mind. She puffed at her cigarette, unable to believe what she was hearing. '– but the officer leading the investigation, Detective Chief Inspector Wise, made the following statement –'

The scene changed. Now Wise stood outside Anson Road, squinting into the sun. 'This *isn't* a reflection on Doctor Fitzgerald's work.' Like hell it isn't, Janice thought. You're just scared he'll show you up. That's what it is, and if you had the balls you'd admit that he's the only one who's ever going to understand me. 'It's a complicated case and we've been forced to use the best resources,' Wise went on. 'Professor Jackson's skills will be invaluable in apprehending the killer of these three men.'

'Two!' Janice screamed at the TV screen.

The picture went back to the newsreader. 'Doctor Fitzgerald was unavailable for comment,' she said.

'You bastards! You stupid, stupid bastards,' Janice screamed. She felt tears running down her cheeks.

She'd always believed she and Fitz were two of a kind. Now she knew she'd been right: no one ever listened to her, and now they'd silenced him, too.

Well, maybe they had. But they weren't going to keep them apart. Not if Janice could do something about it.

Fitz leaned towards the microphone. The heavy professional headphones he was wearing dragged at him uncomfortably, he was vaguely aware of the radio producer on the other side of the glass partition, and of Panhandle next to her. The producer was doing her usual job – soothing callers to *Fitz in Your Face*, his fortnightly phone-in helpline – and, just this once, cueing up a piece of music. Panhandle was there in case the music had the hoped-for effect.

Right now, though, Fitz's attention was on his latest caller. He dragged on his cigarette as she explained the things her husband did to her, had been doing to her for the last five years. 'And he hits you?' he asked.

'Yes,' she whispered. He'd half expected her to tell him that her husband only did those things when she'd made him angry. That would have been the classic syndrome – the victim who'd learned to blame herself for the punishment she was handed out.

She irritated him profoundly. She wanted sympathy. Sympathy would let her continue to be a victim. Well, Fitz wasn't playing. 'But that's all right because he always tells you he loves you afterwards?' he asked gently.

'Yes.'

Fitz leaned back in his chair. 'OK, here's his anniversary present,' he said. 'Take him out for a drink. Take him out for several drinks. Buy him doubles.' Through the partition, Fitz could see the producer frowning at him. But that was OK. Today was one day they couldn't pull him off the air. 'Take him home,' he went on. 'Take him upstairs. When you get to the landing, turn round and push – bump, bump, bump. Deck the bastard. Make *him* lie about the bruises.' The producer was frantic now. She waved her arms desperately at Fitz. 'Then,' Fitz said '– and this is the crucial bit – you tell him you love him.' Behind the producer, Panhandle was grinning her head off. Fitz realised with a doomy feeling that there was a good chance he would lose his job over this. Panhandle's smile almost made it worthwhile. Still, he didn't want to have to tell Judith he'd lost yet another regular source of income. So, for her benefit as much as anyone's, he said, 'There'll be helpline numbers at the end of this programme.' The producer grinned sourly at him. Fitz went on, 'And now for some music. This is dedicated to someone very special.'

The intro started. Fitz closed his eyes and listened. He dragged on his cigarette, and the air filled with smoke. He didn't need to hear the words. He knew them by heart, and though he tried to get ready for the killer's phone call, he couldn't help thinking of Panhandle. *It's the way you make me feel, Whenever I am close to you.* A few millimetres of glass away from him. He could look but not touch. Yet she said she didn't love him, and so she might as well have been light-years away, the glass an uncrossable void –

'Caller for you on line one,' her voice said in his headphones.

Fitz snapped to attention. He flicked the switch on the control desk and picked up the receiver. The transmission light winked out. The public would hear only a rather nice song, and nothing else.

'Doctor Fitzgerald,' he said. Not Fitz, not to her. He wanted as much formality between them as he could muster.

'Why? Why have they taken you off the case?' The voice was echoey. Voice-box, Fitz thought – not that it told him much. Anyone who'd done a bit of physics and could use a soldering iron could make one up.

'Everything was going all right. It doesn't make *sense* –'

If you could call murdering the brightest and best going all right, Fitz thought. 'Difference of opinion,' he said, then cursed himself. Let his revulsion show, let her feel rejected, and she'd be off and running before they could track her down. 'The police aren't the brightest people in the world, you've said so yourself.'

'Yes.' Even through the distortion, there was something in her tone – collusion. She needed to feel they were kindred spirits, then. Needed not love, but understanding.

She didn't speak. He was going to have to lead the conversation. 'Do I get a name?' he asked. He managed to make it sound reasonably like a chat-up line, but she still didn't answer. If he didn't get her talking, he was going to lose her. What did she want? 'I know you better than anyone else but I don't deserve your name?'

'Nina.'

That's something, Fitz thought. Panhandle was recording everything, so he could analyse it later. They'd even hoped someone might recognise the voice, though the distort-box made that unlikely.

'Nina,' he said as gently as he could manage, 'I know you're in pain, I know you're suffering, but –'

She cut in. 'If you're not there and all this is going on, how do they expect to stop it? It'll just go on and on and on.'

That was classic – she didn't feel responsible for what she'd done. It was as if there were two people – the person who loved Fitz and wanted his love and respect and admiration in return; and the person who killed. The person who loved looked on the person who killed and couldn't associate herself with that behaviour. It was as if she merely inhabited the same body as the killer, and could only look on. The trick was to get her to integrate the two sides of herself, so that Nina-who-loved would take responsibility for the actions of Nina-who-killed. And ultimately stop her.

'Stop *you*, Nina. Stop you, not *it*.' There wasn't one chance in a thousand that he'd be able to get through to her now; but all he really wanted was to keep her talking while Wise got to her. He could see Panhandle gesturing at him desperately, but what the bloody hell was she trying to tell him? The killer had gone ominously quiet. He'd have to back off. Give her a direct question. That would get her talking. 'The man in your last letter – did he come round?' he asked. No reply. 'Is there another body?' he demanded.

'They've *got* to put you back on the case.'

Frustration began to take over. 'For his parents' sake, where's the body?'

'He's not dead.' Her impatience came clearly through the distortion.

He knew why that was: he was her great love; he was supposed to understand her, to know not only why she'd done it but – and this was a sign of her psychosis deepening – *what* she'd done. If he could break that down, maybe he could get her to give herself up. At the very least getting an answer would let them move on – let them ruin some poor parents' day, he added to himself. 'Not yet? Or you let him go – which?'

'He's gone,' she said. Relief washed over Fitz. He'd barely realised how frightened he'd been that there'd be another death to lay at his door. He could tell himself that it wasn't his fault till the sun went cold, but there'd still be that guilt, that maybe-if-I'd-done-it-different guilt that would never let him sleep quite as easy as he used to. But Nina was back on her favourite topic. 'You've got to tell them to put you back on the case.'

And suddenly Fitz had had it. 'Nina, you're talking to the wrong guy. You've slaughtered somebody's *children*. Nobody's listening to you any more.' Before he could stop himself, he added, 'Certainly not me.'

'I love you.' The words were distorted by tears as well as the voice-box.

'I can't hear you.' He'd meant it metaphorically, but now he realised it was as good a way of keeping her talking as any.

'I love you.'

More tears. Tough. 'Is it a bad line for you, Nina?' he shouted.

'I love you.' There was a tearing sound. 'I *love* you!' The distortion had gone. That voice, Fitz thought –

The line went dead.

– I know that voice.

Janice took a deep breath and put the phone back on the hook. She went out into the echoing marbled corridor of the main college building, hoping she didn't look as if she'd been crying.

As she started up the stairs to her workroom, she heard feet pounding in the corridor behind her. She turned. Several coppers were heading towards the phone booth. Another student was already using it.

She smiled and went on upstairs. The morning hadn't been a complete washout. She'd told Fitz she loved him. That would work on him, surely. He'd go back to

hat bitch of a wife of his, and he'd realise that he'd be
far better off with someone who really loved him.

And how could anyone love him more than she did?
Who else would have killed to prove it?

THIRTEEN

Frank Weetman stood outside the psychology faculty office. He had his essay in his hand. Steven's essay. There wasn't a lot of point in lying about it to himself. All he had to do was go and put it in. He didn't suppose Janice would tell anyone that he'd stolen it.

He didn't think she cared that much.

But she'd said it was rubbish, a really bad essay.

He turned away from the door. His own essay was in his room. If he was going to fail, he supposed he might as well fail on his own.

Irene Jackson stood in the incident room at Anson Road listening to Detective Chief Inspector Wise brief his men, with a bit of help from Fitz. The words washed over her — something about where she'd posted the letters, and where she'd dumped the bodies, and where that meant she must live — but she couldn't concentrate on them. Not with those photographs in front of her on the wall. Steven Lowry, dead at twenty, his lips twisted by death into a bitter grin they'd never worn in life. She'd known Steven quite well. He'd been in one of her tutorial groups. A kind boy, she'd thought at the time — his essays had always been shot through with an understanding of human nature. He was like Fitz in that regard. She remembered thinking that, too; but, unlike Fitz, Steven had accepted people for what they were, without demanding they strive beyond their abilities to become what they might be. And now there he lay, reduced to pale flesh and staring eyes – a compassionate boy, killed without compassion.

Not that he was perfect, Irene told herself. There was no point idealising the dead. Mourning what they had been was bad enough. There was no point adding perfection to the list.

She tried to look away, but her gaze snagged on the picture of John Branaghan. If anything he was brighter than Steven, though without the younger boy's informing kindness. His last essay had been nothing short of brilliant. If he'd played around, broken a few hearts – and she'd heard that he had – so what? What was twenty-one for, if not to experiment? And now he was just dead, cold clay before his time.

She couldn't stand there and look at him any longer.

'We're going down Regent's Cross,' Wise said. 'Listen to the voice, talk to people –'

'The only students round there don't check out –' Detective Constable Temple objected. He seemed more concerned about the work involved than anything else.

'Well you'll just have to talk to everybody else then, won't you?' Wise said. At least he sounded as if he cared. But to him it was a job. Steven and John weren't people to him, they were cases to be solved. 'On the knocker, house to house,' Wise went on. The police officers groaned.

'Excuse me,' Irene muttered, but nobody seemed to hear her. She pushed her way between the officers. It was just a job to them, and she found she couldn't bear it.

Behind her, Wise said, 'Somebody must've seen Steven Lowry or John Branaghan. Neither of them drove, so check with residents round the bus stops, bus drivers –' She stepped out into the corridor and let the door close behind her, blocking out Wise's voice.

Mark looked just like his photographs, Janice thought as she waited in line. She didn't much like fast food, but just this once she'd decided to make an exception: after all, it was in a good cause.

The bloke in front of her picked up his tray. Mark smiled at him mechanically, and said, 'Have a nice day.'

The man moved away and Janice stepped up to the counter. Mark took her order and tapped it into his till. He scarcely looked at her, but that was OK. She would soon change that. He bustled away to get her food, and she couldn't help noticing that he had a nice arse. Nice eyes, too, like Fitz.

He came back and put the tray on the counter. 'Swiss decaff, medium fries, Chicken Nine Peaks,' he said. 'Three pounds eighty-five, please.'

Janice smiled. She was wearing lipstick, and she had her hair pulled back the way Louise had shown her. Surely he'd think she looked all right. 'Sounds like a Kevin Costner movie,' she said.

Mark looked a bit bewildered. Well, not even Fitz had ever claimed he was very bright.

'Chicken Nine Peaks,' Janice explained.

Mark frowned. 'More like David Lynch, I'd have

167

thought,' he said. 'Enjoy your meal.' He smiled at her.

Smart arse, Janice thought. 'Thanks,' she said. She made a show of looking at his name tag. 'Mark.' She smiled at him, that smile she'd practised over and over again, the smile that stopped her looking so ugly she couldn't bear to look in the mirror; it worked, that smile did. After all, Louise had said it would – 'You could try smiling a bit more. Boys like that.'

Mark seemed to. He smiled back, at any rate, and when she walked away, she was sure he was watching her go.

Irene sat on the toilet. Her hands shook as she took out the quarter bottle of vodka she always kept in her bag. She opened it and knocked back a good slug. Warmth coursed through her. All right, she thought. They're dead. But I'm not. I'm alive. They're dead and that's a dreadful shame, but I'm alive to mourn them.

It was no good. Nothing she could think of brought her any comfort. She couldn't sit here all day. There was someone in the cubicle next to her – even as she thought it, she heard the door open and shut – and anyway, if she didn't go back out soon, people would start to wonder. The sound of running water came from outside.

Irene repressed a sigh and jammed the vodka bottle back in her bag. She stood up and, just for form's sake, flushed the loo.

Then she went outside. Fitz's lady-love – Pentangle or whatever her name was – was washing her hands. Irene thought about leaving before she could say anything, but the girl turned and smiled at her. It would have looked very strange if Irene had just walked out after that, so she went and washed her hands instead.

Pentangle was looking at her. There was something that was close to accusation in her eyes. Irene realised she had to say something. 'Forgive me,' she said. 'It's . . . I taught those boys.' She scrubbed at her hands as if she could scrub away the memory of Steven Lowry's eyes. 'He's very sharp, isn't he – Fitz?'

Pentangle looked at her oddly. Irene wondered if she could smell the booze on her breath. Then she realised that the neck of the bottle of vodka was sticking out of her bag. At least the girl had the good grace not to mention it.

Pentangle went and dried her hands on the towel roll. Irene concentrated on washing her hands. Surely she wouldn't say anything? And what did it matter if she did, half the faculty were on the bottle anyway. Everyone knew that.

'Would you do a television programme tonight?' Pentangle asked from behind her. Irene turned round to face her. 'Standard interview – you refuse to discuss details of the case but you'll talk about the job.'

Irene took a deep breath. She ought to do it. Surely she owed it to John Branaghan. To Steven Lowry. But the thought of it – of being trapped into describing the tortured mind of a person who could do such a thing to them – filled her with dread. 'No,' she said.

'It's working,' Pentangle said. 'Since we put you up front she hasn't killed again.' Fitz had trained her well, Irene thought. That was the one angle she hadn't really considered. How could she refuse to try and save the lives of her other students? And yet, the dread remained. 'We know she's keyed into the television,' Pentangle went on. She was relentless – as relentless in her own way as Fitz was. Irene was beginning to see why she attracted him so much. 'So we need to drive it home that she's not speaking to Fitz any more,' Pentangle finished.

She was right, of course; but still the dread remained, and no rational explanation or need could banish it. 'No,' Irene said again. 'I don't care.' That was a lie. Pentangle stared at her levelly, arms crossed in front of her, her very stance screaming passive aggression. Fitz would have been proud. 'I just can't do this.' That was closer to the truth. 'I can't look at all that . . . stuff, and just carry on.' And still the bloody girl was looking at her as if she was the murderer. Maybe she even had a point, but it just didn't make any difference: what she wanted was beyond what Irene could do. 'You're looking at me like that,' she said, 'but believe me, it's not often I get the chance to say, "I'm the normal one".' Still the crossed arms, the cold-eyed stare. Irene couldn't look at her any more. She pushed the vodka out of sight in her bag, and hoisted it onto her shoulder. 'Tell Fitz I'm sorry,' she said. She headed towards the door. Pentangle moved aside at the last moment, still scowling. 'He shouldn't be too surprised,' Irene added.

She left the toilets and headed down the corridor. She supposed she ought to go back to the university, but the place was full of the stink of death – frightened students masking incipient panic behind loud jokes and stupid graffiti, lecturers too afraid to look each other in the eye, and everybody wondering, 'Did you do it? Did you? Or you?'

She couldn't take it. But she didn't want to go home, either; there she would have to face her own cowardice, her own inability to look into the shadows.

Well, she thought, what else did they make pubs for?

Penhaligon hurried down to meet the rest of the team in the car park. She could hardly believe that Irene Jackson had refused to help.

How could you look at those photos – especially if you'd known the lads in them – and not be moved to do something about it? Yet if you thought that doing that would begin to make you hard, perhaps you would refuse. She knew she'd got a lot tougher in the last couple of years.

She'd cried for Giggsy when he'd been murdered. Cried on the job. When Albie Kinsella knifed Bilborough, she'd done her crying at home.

And Beck – hadn't Jimmy Beck said she was hard? Lacking compassion. She'd thought she was just trying to keep a bit of distance between herself and the job, so she could do her best.

Not that her best was ever quite good enough.

She went out into the car park and saw the rest of the team standing around laughing and joking. All boys together. No worries about compassion for them. No worries about whether they did the job well or not, either. She thought of Alan Temple, and how he'd screwed up when he found Stuart Grady and Bill Nash and thought they were father and son, not lovers. That had cost a man his life, but Alan's response had been to try and get Skelton to take the rap for him.

And that was when the thought that had been in the

back of her mind since Beck's suicide finally crystallised.

I'm going to leave, she thought. I'm a good copper.
I'll be a good something else, instead.

Smiling, she went to join the rest of the team.

Door-to-door. The lads hated the idea and, if he were
honest, Wise wasn't too chuffed himself. But it had to
be done. It was sheer luck their murderer hadn't killed
again; and maybe it was sheer bad luck that had let her
get away when they'd tracked her from her call to the
radio station, but in Wise's opinion it was time to go
back to good, old-fashioned, honest coppering.

Wise stumped along behind the rest of the team as they
headed across the car park. They weren't grumbling now
– they'd save that for when he wasn't around. He
fumbled in his jacket pocket for his car keys. He didn't
mind them moaning, just as long as they got the job
done.

'Trouble up ahead,' Skelton said. He gestured at
something. Temple laughed shortly.

Wise peered between them. Rene was leaning against
his car. She spotted him, and came stalking across the
tarmac towards him, waving a piece of paper. Temple
and Skelton looked at each other, then got out of the
way.

'Who is she?' Rene demanded as soon as Wise got
within screaming distance. Wise saw that the piece of
paper was a credit card statement. 'Thirty-five quid,
Interflora.' She was right up close now. She might be
angry, but he could see she hadn't been sleeping, not if
those dark rings under her eyes were anything to go by.
'Who is she?' Rene demanded again. 'I've stared up at

the ceiling for you.' I always thought you enjoyed it well enough, Wise thought, but Rene carried on before he could get a word in. 'I've raised a child for you.' For *us*, Wise corrected mentally. Rene turned to the others. Jesus, Wise thought. He'd sort of forgotten they were there. 'I stuck with you like a mug. For twenty-five years. For what?' She didn't wait for an answer. 'For this, you shite!'

'Rene,' Wise managed at last, 'the flowers were for *you*!'

She pulled an insulted face. 'So what am I now? Alzheimers? You think I wouldn't remember flowers?'

Wise stepped up close to her. If he could have, he'd have asked her to come somewhere private to talk, but there just wasn't the time. He made do with lowering his voice. 'They were booked in advance for our silver wedding, you silly mare.' She frowned. Maybe he was getting to her. 'Work's busy,' he said. 'I didn't want to forget, right? You were *meant* to get 'em tomorrow.'

She pursed her lips. Looked away from him. 'You're lying,' she said.

'Check!' Wise said, beginning to lose his temper. 'Check with the bloody florist!'

'No bloody point if I have to check, is there?' She started to walk away. Wise reached to grab her arm, but she shook him off.

'Get in the car, Rene,' he said. He thought of spending another night avoiding Mrs Johnson at the guest house. Of all the nights he might have to spend in places like that. 'We'll talk. We'll sort it out.'

Tears glinted on her cheeks. 'Tonight,' she said. 'The house. If you've got anything worth saying.'

She turned and left before Wise could say anothe word.

The girl was waiting for Mark when he got off work Somehow he'd known she would be. There'd bee something in the way she looked at him – maybe it wa the fact that she'd checked his name.

He came out of the BurgerMeister with the res of his shift, and she was sitting on the seats in th square outside, smoking. She smiled when she saw him a million-watt smile that chased off the memory o the smell of industrial-strength mayonnaise and ho vegetable oil.

'Hiya,' he said. His mate Pete raised an eyebrow a him, but followed the others down the road.

'Again,' she said.

Mark went over to her. 'You waiting for someone? he asked, knowing she wasn't.

She pointed to a battered red van that was parked u at the side of the road with its hazard lights flashing 'RAC,' she said. 'Starter motor keeps packing up.' She grinned again. It lit her face up. 'Don't suppose you're any good with cars?'

'Not a bit,' Mark said. He realised the others were going on without him. 'We're meant to be off down the Boardwalk.'

'Go on then,' she said, cool as you like.

'Good luck.' He started to leave, but he couldn't quite take his eyes off her. It was her smile that did it, he thought. The smile, the eyes. He wasn't even going to let himself think about the tits.

'OK,' she said.

He got about three yards down the road. The others were disappearing round the corner. Idiot, he thought. You berk, Mark. You should at least get her number.

He turned round and went back. 'You want to try pushing it?'

'OK,' she said. 'If it works, I could give you a lift.'

Yeah, Mark thought, looking at her legs, thinking about her tits. *Yeah*.

FOURTEEN

Judith got some ice out of the freezer for her gin and tonic. It was almost civilised – her and Fitz in the kitchen, pretending to talk, Katie in the front room pretending to do her homework. Almost but not quite. She wandered across the kitchen – knowing what she was about to do she couldn't bear to stand too close to Fitz – and checked her watch.

'You off out, then?' he asked.

It was too much to hope that he hadn't noticed that she was dressed to go out. She just prayed he hadn't realised how nervous she was. She glanced at him and smiled, but she couldn't quite look him in the eye. 'Yes. James is staying with my mother.' He scowled. 'No offence.' If she were lucky, maybe he wouldn't bring up the fact that not so long ago she was the one who couldn't be trusted to look after James.

'Where?' There was naked hostility in the question.

'Well I don't know where exactly. We're all meeting at the office.' She was a rotten liar, and Fitz knew it. When they'd first met, it had been a joke between them: that no one could keep a secret from Fitz, but that Judith was so bad at it that he didn't need to be a psychologist to ferret out whatever she was hiding. It had made them laugh, once.

It wasn't a laughing matter now.

'So if your baby gets sick and your mother gets worried and she phones me, I'm to say "I'm sorry, they all met at the office and we haven't a clue where they're eating"?' Fitz demanded. He crossed the kitchen and stood very close to her. She was in his shadow, now; how strange, she thought, when things are going all right, I love the size of him. It's a comfort to me. But now he just intimidates me. It wasn't just his physical size though. It was his intellect, and the way he'd use it to cut through to the heart of any problem.

'I'll ring and leave a number when . . .' she faltered. She was lying to him. For God's sake, why shouldn't he be angry when she was lying to him? But she thought of Danny, of his earnestness, of his fear that she would hurt him. Fitz had had more than enough chances to make his end of the marriage work, and as far as she could see, though he liked to say how much of a damn he gave, the words never got translated into actions. 'I'll ring with a number when I know where we're eating. All right?' she said. She gulped at her gin. He knew she was lying. Of course he did. 'For God's sake, why are you trying to make me feel guilty for going out on my own for the second time since James was born?'

That was a mistake. She knew it before he even said a word. 'I don't know, Judith – when was the first?' He wasn't shouting. She could have dealt with his shouting, if only by walking out. 'Look at me,' he said quietly.

Judith felt her fingers go tight on her glass. Unwillingly, she looked at him. There was anger in his eyes, but also despair. She knew she ought to say something,

178

out the only things she could say would make him call her out on her lies. It's over, she thought. Whatever happens now – whether I see Danny tonight or not, whether I sleep with him tonight or next week or never – there's no going back from this moment.

The only question in her mind was whether he'd worked out who she was going to see.

I have to say something, she thought desperately.

Katie saved her. She hesitated at the kitchen door, carrying a piece of paper. 'Dad, you've got a fax coming through,' she said. She sounded puzzled. 'It says, "The man who's coming to dinner ..."' she read from the page.

It made no sense to Judith, but Fitz slammed his drink down on the worktop. 'Christ,' he muttered. He left without explaining, and ran upstairs.

Judith followed him more slowly. She'd had an awful thought – supposing someone had decided to tell Fitz about her and Danny? But who? And why would Fitz react like this? There was nothing to implicate either of them in that one –

'Oh God, NO!' Fitz bellowed. Judith raced up the stairs. She found him standing by the fax machine. There were a couple of pages in his hand.

'What?' she demanded 'What is it?'

He didn't answer. She went over and took the papers from his clenched fingers. 'Long dark hair, brown eyes like his dad, about five feet nine and a kind face with a nice name ...' said the first sheet. The second said, 'Mark. That's a nice name, isn't it?'

'What is it, Fitz,' Judith demanded. 'Tell me! What's happened to him?'

But it was Fitz's turn to be unable to answer.

Penhaligon rapped on DCI Wise's office door, but went in without waiting to be told to. Wise had his jacket on – his smart jacket, she noted, and a fresh shirt and tie. There was a bunch of flowers on the desk. A big bunch.

Penhaligon smiled, hoping for his sake it would be enough.

'Can I have a word, please, sir?' she said.

'Make it snappy, Jane, I've got to be somewhere,' he said. He seemed happier than he had in days.

'This won't take a minute, sir,' she answered. 'I just wanted to give you this.' She took a deep breath and handed him an envelope.

He tore it open. 'If this is a joke it's not a very funny one,' he said when he read the contents.

'No, sir,' she said. 'I've thought about it a lot – about everything that happened with me and Jimmy Beck – and this is what I want.'

'All right,' Wise said. 'But do me a favour – take a few days to think about it again. You might feel different then.'

When Fitz wasn't around, he meant. 'If you insist, sir,' she said. 'But I don't think it'll make a difference.'

'OK, Jane.' He made a point of putting the envelope at the bottom of the pile of work in his in-tray.

'Goodnight, sir,' she said.

She went back out into the incident room, feeling like a prisoner who's suddenly been given a free pardon.

She'd almost got to the outer door when the phone rang.

● ● ●

anice. Her name was Janice. She tasted of cigarettes
nd peaches, and she wanted him far more than Mark
ad dared to hope.

It was like something out of a book, he thought as his
ingers tangled in her hair. Beautiful older woman – and
he was beautiful, though she'd laughed when he'd told
er that – picks up teenager in dead-end job and takes
im home for . . . what? A night of wild sex, or some-
hing more? Mark didn't know whether he wanted that
r not. He hadn't been out with anyone since Debbie.
Iadn't been to bed with anyone, come to that.

He kissed her gently at first, then fiercely. She leaned
nto him, pinning him to the sofa. Her hands moved
lown his back, to his arse, and then up, under his tee
hirt. He felt her nipples pressing into his chest, hard as
ullets, and he moved his hands down to explore
hem, but he was thinking, I shouldn't be doing this, I
hould –

– and she pulled away.

'Hang on,' he said, glad of the chance to think for a
noment.

She laughed and backed away from him, but she held
er hand out. 'Why?' she said. 'It's what you came for.'

He wanted to say, but I hardly know you, but the
nemory of her scent and the pressure of her lips against
is tantalised him.

The tips of her fingers trailed against his arm. It sent
hivers up him. He wanted her so much, and it had been
o long since he'd done this.

With good reason, he told himself. But the promise of
hose eyes, those lips . . . he stood up and reached for
er. She backed off, still laughing and went through a

door. He went after her. It was like walking into a little
girl's room – all sugary pink and full of stuffed toys
with a single bed covered in a flowery duvet.

'Have you got a kid?' he asked. 'Do you share?' The
room just didn't match her attitude – randy as hell and
willing to go out and get what she wanted.

She just smiled and led him across the room. She
pulled back a curtain, and he saw there was another
room beyond the first. She pulled him by the hand, and
when he held back, she turned it over and kissed the
tender place on the inside of his wrist.

As she pulled him through into the inner room he
said, 'Look, I haven't got anything.' She isn't going to
take no for an answer, he thought. 'I'm not carrying
anything,' he said, but it didn't sound convincing even
to him. For an answer she wrapped herself around him
and kissed him hard. She broke off and went to close
the curtain. He stared round at the room. It was like
a Goth's dream of heaven – all wrought iron and
lit candles, despite the daylight filtering through the
venetian blinds that masked the windows. 'I'm doing
nothing without a rubber,' he said. There was never
going to be another Debbie in his life.

She came back and laid her finger gently on his lips.
'It's all right, Mark,' she said. She grabbed him by the
arms and started backing towards the bed, with its drifts
of snowy pillows. She was holding him tight – too
tight, and he didn't like it. He stood his ground. 'You're
shaking,' he said. It was true. He could feel her hands
trembling despite the force of her grip.

'I've got some,' she said.

'You're shaking,' he said again. He didn't want her

aying afterwards that he'd taken advantage of her.

'It's all right,' she said again, and sat down on the bed. She lay back and drew him down on top of her.

'I don't want to do this,' he said. She started to put her arms around him. He could feel her breath hot on his face. The scent of her . . . he fought to get his arms under him.

'It's OK,' she said soothingly, and part of him wanted to take what she was offering.

'I just don't want to do this,' he said, and pulled free of her. He stood up, not knowing what to say to her or how to explain his reluctance. His body wanted her, all right. It was his head that was having the problems.

'What's the matter with me?' she screamed at him. Her face was a mask of rage. 'Not good enough?' She was suddenly ugly.

He backed away from her, towards the curtains. Look, let's cool it down,' he said. He tried to find a way to let her down gently. 'I can give you a ring and we can work stuff out.' He tried a smile. She glared at him. He backed a way a bit further. 'You're really nice,' he lied, thinking that she was really desperate, really crazy – the way she'd suddenly turned, and the way she was staring at him, like she hated him. 'It's a nice place.' Another lie. It was creepy – the other bedroom with the teddy bears, this one with the candles lit in the daytime, like she'd gone out looking for someone to bring home. He kept moving back. 'I'm – It's me. All right?' He was almost at the curtain now. His hand brushed against it. 'It's me –' he said again, and turned. He yanked the curtain back.

His father's face stared down at him – the huge poster

for his radio show, and black and white snaps of Da‹
with Mum, Dad with that bit on the side of his, Dad an‹
Katie. His Dad and Mark himself.

'What the fuck?' he said, turning back to Janice.

He saw the tyre iron coming down at his head and h‹
couldn't do a thing about it. It filled his vision, and the‹
pain sliced through him, and the world went red aroun‹
him.

FIFTEEN

They drove to Anson Road police station in total silence: Judith next to Fitz in the back, Penhaligon – he seemed pale and tired – next to DCI Wise in the front.

There was nothing to say, Judith thought. Mark might be dead by now, or in pain. And Fitz seemed to have guessed that her night out was far from business.

She stared out the window and tried not to cry.

Pain dragged Mark from unconsciousness. He lay for a moment with his eyes closed. He felt nauseous, and his arms were at an odd angle. There was something warm and wet on his forehead, something cold and wet on his wrists. He could make no sense of any of it.

He opened his eyes slowly. At first all he could see was a blur of red and grey. The world emerged slowly – swathes of sheer curtains, candlelight flickering in gathering darkness, the rails of a black iron bedstead. The huge poster of Fitz staring down at him from the opposite wall. It took him a moment or two to remember the cosh coming down at his head.

Janice.

She'd wanted him to go to bed with him. That was it. Yes. And she'd had photographs of Dad. Her face had been like a mask of hatred.

He tried to bring his arms down to his sides. Chains rattled, but he couldn't move. His legs were held, too. He twisted his head round. He was handcuffed to the bedframe. Gel glistened on his wrists.

She'd stripped him naked.

Christ, he thought.

He yanked hard at the chains. The cuffs bit into his wrists. Panic surged through him. He took a long, ragged breath and tried to force himself to be calm.

Piano music started to play. Nothing he recognised, some crappy old vinyl, by the sound of it. He levered himself up as far as he could, and caught sight of Janice half concealed behind a partition wall on the far side of the room.

'What are you doing?' he said, and was surprised and pleased at how calm he sounded. A sex game, he thought. That's what it is. Some stupid sex game. She hasn't really hurt me, she just let it get a bit out of hand because she was angry at me. That's it.

'Shut up,' she said. Her voice was flat. Emotionless. It frightened him almost more than anything else that had happened.

Not a sex game, then. It had been a stupid thing to hope, anyway, especially with those pictures of his dad on the wall. He realised he was cold, and wondered if it was fear. He might be concussed or something, though he could see well enough now.

What would Dad say? Talk. That was his answer to everything. Same thing the women's self-defence instructor had told Debbie. He remembered her telling him about it – 'She said, talk first and if that doesn't

ork, kick 'em in the bollocks.' But it hadn't really
een a joke – the idea was that they couldn't hurt you if
ou were a real human being.

OK, he thought. I can do this. She seemed to like me
t first. I can do this. But he was trembling. He could
arely swallow, let alone talk.

Janice came through the doorway in the partition
all. She was pulling a trolley laden with electrical
ear.

'What're you *doing*?' She didn't answer. 'Janice?'
lis voice was shaking. 'Look at me.' But she wouldn't.
he vocals cut in on the record. *It isn't the way that you
ook, And it isn't the way that you talk.* The voice was
aunting, lonely. 'Has he done something to you?'
Mark demanded. '*Look at me!*'

She did then, and he saw that she was crying. The
ears made silvery tracks in her make-up.

'Are you one of his patients?' he asked. Wrong. Her
xpression changed from misery to contempt. She made
derisive noise. OK, if that was an insult . . . 'You're
friend?' She ignored him and started to unroll an
lectrical flex from the trolley. What the fuck was she
oing to do? 'A good friend?' he went on. Keep talking,
e thought. Sooner or later she's got to answer back.
hen I'm in with a chance. 'Has he let you down? It
ouldn't surprise me.' Christ, he thought, I wish he was
ere now. Janice plugged the flex in. What's she going
o do? The question screamed through Mark's mind. He
elt his pulse hammering at his wrists. He swallowed.
ot to stay calm. Doesn't matter what she's going to do,
nly that she doesn't actually do it. 'He's not . . . he can
e a bit of a twat sometimes . . .' he said. Janice came

187

back to the trolley. She picked up something. 'I can ta[l]
to him,' he said quickly. She started towards him. H[e]
saw that the object was a packing tape dispenser. 'I ca[n]
get him to talk to you and you can tell him about it and [I]
won't say anything.' he said. She stood over him for [a]
second. Then she tore a length of tape off the roll. '[I]
won't say anything,' he said again.

She slammed the tape against his mouth, and pulled i[t]
tight, silencing him. He stared up at her, but there wa[s]
only fury in her eyes. He slumped back against th[e]
pillows with the sound of his own laboured breathin[g]
loud in his ears.

'He doesn't care what you think,' Janice screame[d]
'You don't even *talk* to each other properly, so don'[t]
give me that shit.'

Mark could scarcely breathe for terror.

'Don't pretend you've got a direct line, Mark.' Sh[e]
went back to the trolley and picked up a clamp. A re[d]
clamp, attached to the trolley by an electrical flex. Sh[e]
clipped it to the head of the bedstead.

Christ, Mark thought. She's going to electrocute me.

'I have,' she said. She picked up a black clamp an[d]
went to the foot of the bed.

Mark realised his cheeks were wet with tears. H[e]
turned his head away, but he couldn't block out he[r]
voice.

'He'll have to look at me now, won't he?' she sai[d]
'Now I'm really special.'

And through her tears, she smiled.

SIXTEEN

Fitz looked terrible. The harsh television lights turned his skin pallid, and his eyes were raw-looking. Next him at the table, DCI Wise had started the press release: 'We are appealing to anyone who might've seen Mark since he left work at 8.00 p.m. to come forward immediately,' he said in his flat Liverpudlian accent. All the time he spoke, Fitz's finger – just his finger, nothing else – moved against the table top. It made Janice want to weep. How could they have put him through this? First they fired him, then they dragged him through this. 'Especially in the vicinity of Regent Cross,' Wise continued. 'He could have been travelling with a young woman, possibly slightly older than himself, possibly answering to the name, "Nina".'

That was her. They were talking about her. The thought sent a little chill of satisfaction down Janice's spine. Of course, they hadn't figured out that it wasn't her real name, but that was because they'd taken Fitz off the case. Her Fitz. He was thinking about her now, about how to make her listen to him.

But the cost of it. He looked dreadful – pale and washed-out, as if he'd been living with the loss of Mark for weeks, rather than just less than an hour. But it would be all right. He'd find her, and she would comfort him. She would make it be all right, and they'd never be parted again. Once he'd realised how greatly she loved him, he wouldn't let anyone take her away from him.

Yet she couldn't deny how awful he looked. She realised she was crying for him. Someone had to. His wife didn't care, and that frigid bitch Penhaligon wasn't much better – she was obviously just using him. Let him solve the cases while she took the credit. She'd probably been the one that got him kicked off the case.

Janice swiped at her eyes with the back of her hand. It came away covered in tears.

But Fitz was talking and she was missing it. She forced herself to listen quietly. '. . . I beg you, please just *talk* to him, Nina,' he said. 'Mark's a good listener, just talk to him. Let him ring us. Or you could ring us to let us know he's . . .' he breathed in hard. 'That he's . . .' he tried again. 'I beg you please don't hurt him, Nina.'

'Oh God! Look what they've done to you,' she whispered. Couldn't they see how they were hurting him, stripping him of his dignity, making him sit up there and tear his soul apart for all to see?

'Please, Nina,' he said, 'I beg you, just don't hurt him . . .' The last words were muffled in sobs.

The picture went dark, and was replaced by the Anson Road police station phone number.

Janice reached over and turned the television off. 'Soon,' she whispered. 'Soon it'll all be over, Fitz.'

Mark lay in darkness pierced by the flickering flames of a hundred candles.

He had to work at breathing, and his harsh gasping

was counterpointed by the click, click, clicking of the timer counting down the moments until a thousand volts of electricity would surge through his body.

Fitz sat in the incident room nursing a cup of stale coffee. He had to concentrate to stop his fingers plunging straight through the plastic cup, but that was OK. It helped to keep the memory of John Branaghan's body — stiff white flesh and blind, burst eyes accusing the sky, and that death-grin on his face mocking the still living — from his mind; because when he saw it, it had Mark's face, and Mark's face was the one wearing that terrible smile as his muscles were locked forever by the searing lance of electricity.

'Tell me what she'd done to the others,' Judith said from beside him. It was the first thing she'd said since he'd come out of the press conference. Wise had wanted her in there with him, but Fitz had vetoed that: Nina wanted to talk to him. Only the hope that she could use Mark as a bargaining counter to achieve that aim was keeping Mark alive. If he were alive. 'Exactly what she's done,' Judith repeated.

He could feel Judith's hysteria, tamped down tight but still there under the thin skin of her self-control. One word from him and she'd break.

He couldn't cope with that.

He could barely handle his own panic.

'Don't,' he said, staring hard at the coffee, seeing Mark's face in the scum that floated on its surface. Nothing he could say would offer her any comfort. If he could have found a lie to tell her, he would have. God knows they'd told each other enough lies in the course

191

of their marriage that one more wouldn't make a jot of difference. But what could he tell her – that Nina's victims died fast, that they never felt a thing?

Wise came over with fresh coffee. Fitz heard Judith's muttered 'No', and was glad that the DCI didn't offer him any. He was conscious of Wise's shadow falling over him, of the man's indecision.

Don't say anything, he thought. He was like Judith. One word of kindness and he'd have broken.

Panhandle saved him. She appeared in the doorway that led to the communications' room. 'Sir! She's on the line.'

Fitz went past her at a dead run, and grabbed the receiver off a tense-looking civilian clerical officer. He took a couple of long, deep breaths before he dared speak into the phone.

Judith was right behind him. He could feel the force of her expectation like a physical weight, bearing down on him. I can do this, he thought. All those others he'd broken down – Tina and her lover Shaun who blew himself to pieces, Cassidy, Kenneth Trant with his God-fixation. Jimmy Beck. None of them meant a thing, compared with what he had to do now.

He tried to get into Nina's mindset. Youngish. Low self-esteem – so low she'd go for an old fat clever guy the way he'd wanted Panhandle to. Desperate for attention. Focus on that need, on the fact that this is a cry for help. So how can I help her? What kind of attention is she so lacking? He'd know within minutes of speaking. He put the handset to his ear, and prepared to flatter her. It would be a beginning. But when he spoke, the first thing he said was, 'It's Fitz. Where is he?'

'Are you all right?' Nina asked. The voice was familiar, but he couldn't place it.

'Is he alive?' Sod psychology. He had to know.

'Have they said you can have your job back?' Nina asked. She sounded genuinely concerned.

'Is Mark *alive*?'

'Yes.' Thank God, Fitz thought, even as he registered the impatience in her voice, as if she were disposing of the unimportant business so they could have a nice chat. Fitz felt Judith collapse against him. Her fingers dug into his arm.

It took everything Fitz had left, but he managed to say, 'What exactly is it you want, Nina?'

Keep her talking, he thought. If he couldn't do anything else, it would give Wise time to get a location on her phone number.

'I want you.' It was ludicrous. No more ludicrous than any of the other cases he'd ever dealt with, but he just couldn't do it, couldn't make that leap of the imagination that would allow him to follow her twisted logic.

'I have a question for you, Nina,' he said.

'OK.' She sounded excited. This was what she had wanted: his undivided attention. But a bright first-year student could have figured that much out. He needed the deeper reasons, the why beneath the why. But all that raged through him was the need to find Mark, to protect him.

'If you hurt Mark, could you see us hitting it off?' It was as much as he could do not to scream it at her. If he'd had her there, he'd have been tempted to beat it out of her.

His anger had never been physical, not for all the temper tantrums he'd thrown. It frightened him. But not as much as the prospect of seeing Mark dead on a mortuary slab.

Nina didn't answer.

'You'd be letting yourself down,' Fitz said. If she thought he was angry it might drive her to put the phone down. Might make her do something really stupid. What did she want? Attention? She had attention. It didn't seem to be enough. Why was she doing this? And suddenly he felt that little leap of understanding: she didn't know herself. He'd lay odds on it. 'You'd never hear what I've got to say to you,' he said. It was too much for Fitz. He couldn't hold the panic down any longer. 'So it's not in your interests to hurt my son, is that clear?'

'That's one way of looking at it,' Nina said. She sounded puzzled.

She really doesn't think Mark's life is of any importance compared to the relationship she imagines herself having with me, Fitz thought. It was the biggest clue he'd got to her behaviour so far. He licked his lips and said, 'You were at my lecture on Monday?'

'Yes,' she murmured. Her voice was soft now, and full of wonder, as if they were about to make love for the first time.

'Love and sex and devotion – are you looking for all those things?'

'Yes,' she said. He could almost feel her smiling down the phone at him.

This was better. If he could make her think he was on her side – that it was the two of them against a hostile world – perhaps he could cajole where Mark was out of her.

The line went dead.

'What?' he said. 'Oh God, I've lost her –' What had he said? Had he angered her? Was she, even now, preparing to take her anger out on Mark? Maybe thinking they'd tracked her down, that she'd have to kill him and get rid of the body?

Had he said something wrong? *Was it his fault?*

He heard a noise behind him, and whirled round. Wise and Panhandle were looking at him. 'What have you done?' he demanded, shaking the phone's handset at them.

'I cut her off,' Wise said calmly.

'So long as I'm talking to her,' Fitz bellowed. 'The boy stays alive. You cut her off, she panics.' Wise just stood there and took it. That just made Fitz angrier. 'As long as she's got my boy, you do not make her panic!'

'She was ringing from a mobile,' Wise said when Fitz had stopped.

'That's Mark's,' Judith said. She clutched at Fitz's shoulder. 'I can ring him.'

'No,' Wise said. 'I cut her off.' Fitz glared at him, though he'd already worked out where they were going with this. 'We can only trace a mobile to a radius,' Wise explained. Light bounced off his glasses, making his expression hard to read. 'Now she's desperate, she'll use a call box. We'll force her out.'

It was the same argument Fitz had used. He followed the logic of it, but he hated it all the same, hated losing his only contact with his son, however tenuous; hated, if he were honest, admitting that Wise was right.

195

'You stupid bastard,' he snarled.

'We know which one we think she uses,' Wise said. 'But there are four more in Regent Cross. We're covering them all.'

'He's right,' Panhandle added quietly.

Fitz looked at her, and then away. He couldn't meet her eyes, not with Judith in the room. Not when he needed her to help save his family.

'Well find him,' Judith wailed. She came round from behind Fitz and stood between him and Wise. 'This is what you do. It's what you say you do.' She whirled to face Fitz, and jabbed her finger at him. 'It's the only thing *you* say you do that I believe in.' She balled her fist up and made to hit Fitz. But she didn't. 'So bloody well *find* him.' She collapsed against Fitz, and began to sob.

The phone in Wise's office began to ring.

Wise yanked the receiver off the phone. Fitz was right behind him, with Judith standing next to him, her face smeared from crying.

'Wise,' he said. Jesus, he thought, what has she got X-ray vision? How the hell else could she have got this number?

'Charlie?' Rene's voice said.

The breath went out of Wise in one great rush. He shook his head at Fitz and Judith. 'Rene?' Wise said, as much to let them know what was going on as anything else.

Fitz's jaw worked. He put his arm round Judith, and they left together. The door slammed after them.

'You said you'd be round tonight,' Rene said. 'To talk, you said.'

'Well, I will,' Wise answered. Part of him wanted to smile, just because he was talking to her. 'But something's come up at work –'

'Something always does,' Rene snapped.

'I'm here, aren't I?' Wise demanded. 'I'm not out gallivanting, am I?'

'Well, no . . .' She sounded dubious. 'But –'

'But nothing – a kid's been kidnapped. He'll be murdered if we don't find him.' He waited. She didn't say anything. 'Now, do you want me to come and talk to you or what?'

'No.' Again, silence. Wise could feel his marriage slipping away into that silence. 'I just wanted to say –' she hesitated. He could imagine her mouth going tight as she tried to say something she didn't like, 'I checked with the florist, you see . . . so I wanted to say I'm sorry.'

He meant to say, and was it worth it? If you had to check, was it worth it? But all he could manage was, 'Oh.'

'Look,' she said, 'when you get things sorted out there, you come round. It doesn't matter what time.'

Wise couldn't find anything to say. He licked his lips. Say something, you stupid bastard, he thought at himself. 'What are you saying?' he managed at last.

'I'm saying I want us to sort things out. We'll see a counsellor, if we have to . . .' Don't say it, Wise thought. 'Maybe that Fitz bloke,' she went on. 'He was very good.'

'Maybe,' Wise said. 'But it's his son that's been kidnapped.'

'Oh God,' Rene said. 'Well, don't just stand there – go and sort it out.'

'Well, I will,' Wise said. 'I'll see you later, all right?'

'All right,' Rene said.

Wise put the phone down. When he went outside [to] the others, it was all he could do to stop himse[lf] grinning.

Temple and Skelton sat in an unmarked car with its ligh[ts] off, watching the phone box on the corner opposite.

This is it, Temple thought as the woman approache[d.] My chance to make good. He picked up the handset [of] his car radio. 'Woman approaching,' he said. 'Abou[t] five-five, early thirties. Blonde, medium build . . .' G[o] on, he thought. Go in. But she walked straight past. 'N[o] call,' he said. 'She's gone past.'

He slammed the receiver down.

Judith sat watching Fitz smoke. She hated it. Hated th[e] smell of it, the way it clung to his clothes, the way h[e] tasted of it on those rare occasions when they still mad[e] love.

But she was so glad of him being there – of his shee[r] physical presence. Of the fact that he knew her s[o] well. He might not always make her happy, and h[e] hadn't always been there when she needed him, but thi[s] time . . . at least this time he was there.

She had never felt closer to him.

He looked at her. She wanted to ask him to hold he[r] but even now she couldn't do it.

He pushed the phone across the desk to her. 'Don'[t] you want to phone and tell your friends why you'r[e] late?' he asked.

She thought he'd forgotten. God, she thought. Mar[k]

may be dead and I'm sitting here hoping he's forgotten
he'd worked out I was seeing someone else.

And she knew then: no matter how nice it was,
having Danny doting on her, holding her, making her
feel cherished and wanted – no matter all that. What she
needed was Fitz making demands on her, Fitz loving
her in his own, special, screwed-up way.

Fitz understanding her.

'It doesn't matter,' she said. 'Not now.'

Danny Fitzgerald sat at his table in the Red Pagoda. She
will come, he told himself. She said she was taking me
seriously. He checked his watch. Nine-fifteen. She was
over an hour late.

He caught the waiter's eye and ordered another lager.

She will come, he told himself again; but there was a
coldness in his heart that made him know he was
fooling himself.

The clicking of the timer was the only sound that broke
the silence. Mark lay listening to it, forcing himself to
breathe slowly. He could feel his pulse at his ankles and
wrists.

The candles were beginning to gutter and die, and the
light falling through the windows had long since faded.

How much longer? he wondered.

Hot water sluiced over Janice. She stepped out of
the shower and wrapped herself in her fluffiest towel,
imagining that Fitz was holding it out for her, wrapping
t round her, patting her gently dry.

She went into the bedroom and sat in front of the

dressing table, blow-drying her hair. I wish I were pretty, she thought, looking at herself. Maybe then things would have been different. I *am* pretty, she thought defiantly, looking at the wide-set dark eyes, the neat nose . . . Steven Lowry had said she was pretty; so had John Branaghan, and Frank Weetman. And Mark - Mark had called her beautiful.

Well, they were just wrong, weren't they? They were boys, and stupid with it. A man would have known she wasn't pretty. That was why she had to be so careful - get the hair just right, the make-up perfect – anything to disguise her plainness.

Louise had laughed at her when she'd said that. What had her words been? 'I'm not the pretty one, Janice - you are!' Laughing at her, trying to see if she'd fall for it.

Well, she hadn't fallen for it. She knew what she was.

She attacked her hair with the brush and hairdryer, forcing it to curl, just so. She pushed it back off her face. Her eyes were her best feature – that's what people said – and she wanted to make the most of them.

Next, the dress. It was one of Louise's favourites, which Janice had begged off her. It wasn't like the ones she'd worn for John Branaghan and Frank Weetman. They were boys. They only understood blatant sexiness: show them a girl in a short dress with a plunge neckline and they'd be on top of her in ten seconds. Fitz was a *man*. The dress she'd chosen was subtle – black silk, not clinging but cut to move with her as she walked. It buttoned down the front, and she left it open at the neck, just enough to get Fitz's imagination work

g. Jewellery – demure earrings and a heavy gold necklace, long enough to dip almost to her breasts. It could direct his eye, she thought; she knew enough about body language and what clothing could imply to know that. Shoes – she was tempted by the stilettoes he'd worn for John Branaghan, but in the end she lumped for medium-heeled black velvet. She didn't want to look tarty.

Finally, the make-up. A touch of foundation. No blusher, but mascara, and a little eye-shadow to emphasise her dark eyes. Then lipstick. Cherry Flame. Kiss me, Fitz, she thought as she applied it. Kiss me . . .

She looked at herself in the mirror. I'm not ugly, she told herself. I'm not.

Soon, perhaps, Fitz would tell her that himself.

She went to the phone and sat down. She was shaking so much with excitement that she could barely hold the phone. She took a moment to compose herself, and then she punched the number.

'I want to speak to Fitz,' she said when she got through. 'Tell him it's me.'

A moment later, he came on the line. 'Yes? Fitz.'

'No,' Janice said. 'In person.' She put the phone down.

Then she waited.

It took about three minutes for Fitz, Judith and Wise's team to pile into cars and head for Nina's flat.

It seemed to take for ever.

Fitz sat in the back with Judith while Panhandle drove. They screamed down the road after a marked car, with their own portable light and siren wailing.

None of them said a word. Fitz watched Judith i
the rearview mirror. Her hands were still in her la
clenched round a rag of paper tissue. Only a muscl
jumping in her jaw gave her tension away.

They pulled up outside a row of old shops. Yellov
light from a single streetlamp bounced off their blin
windows and boarded-up fronts. Temple was waitin
for them, next to a police van.

Wise was out first. 'Is she there?' he asked.

Fitz clambered out as fast as his bulk would let him
'Yeah,' he heard Temple say. 'She is.'

He didn't say that, Fitz thought as he ran for th
doorway, with Judith hurrying to keep up beside him
He did *not* imply that my son is not up there.

The stairs loomed ahead of him. He took them thre
at a time, but even so a couple of uniformed copper
were ahead of him. The front door stood open. H
went in.

She was in the living room. As he went in, she turne
to face him. Her lipsticked smile lit up her face. Wher
had he seen her before? He knew he'd seen her. Christ
the way she was looking at him . . . it reminded him o
the way a baby who has been parted from its mothe
smiles when at last it sees her again. Totally imprinted
He logged the information in his mind in case h
needed it again – he feared he would, though he hope
he wouldn't.

'Mark?' Judith called from beside him again. 'Mark?'

There was desperation in her voice. She'd obviousl
worked out what Fitz had known as soon as he walke
in: this many coppers would surely have found Mark b
now. She ran across to one of the doors leading out o

202

he living room, but he still couldn't take his eyes off
Nina.

That wasn't her name. He was sure of it. He just
couldn't place her face. He forced himself to look round
the room, to find out what he could about her from it.
But it was bland, dull. A room belonging to someone
who had tried to erase herself, to make herself nothing.
That in itself was worth noting. Maybe she had such
low self-esteem that she thought that was the only way
people would accept her. It would fit one type of serial
killer pattern, at any rate.

'Mark,' Judith screamed. She sounded on the verge
of panic.

My God, Fitz thought. I'm standing here looking at
this bloody cow instead of . . . he crossed the room to
the room Judith hadn't explored. As he did so, Nina
twisted round in her seat so she could keep looking at
him.

For the first time in his life, Fitz looked at someone he knew to be mentally unstable and thought,
that's creepy, the way he knew an untrained person
would.

Even in the middle of his rising panic, he thought at
himself – liar. It was what had attracted him to psychology in the first place: looking at pictures of killers in the
paper and thinking, creepy! And knowing that the way
to exorcise them was to understand them.

All of that, in the two strides it took him to get to the
doorway, with Nina's crazy eyes on him.

He walked into a child's bedroom. That was his first
impression – rosebud wallpaper, soft toys piled on
shelves and on the end of the bed, an expensive-

looking doll's house complete with furniture. Only the cosmetics scattered across the dressing table told him that this was, indeed, Nina's room.

To hell with analysis.

He wanted Mark.

He crossed the room in two strides. Looked under the bed. A divan – no space there. In the wardrobe? He yanked the doors open and riffled through the clothes. Nothing.

Judith flicked aside a curtain. Light poured in from the street outside. She turned and ran to the living room. Fitz tried to stop her but he was too late. Wise and Panhandle dived at her.

'I want to speak to her,' Judith shouted. She stretched hands like claws past Wise and Panhandle. Fitz dodged round them. 'I just want to speak to her.'

Fitz got up close to Nina. He leaned on the arms of her chair. 'If they let her through she's going to kill you,' he said.

'You'll just have to protect me, Fitz,' Nina answered. She was all wide-eyed innocence, and she said the words as if what she'd suggested were their own private joke.

Dammit, he did know her . . . but still the face eluded him.

'Where is he?' he shouted.

She stared up at him, a defiant little girl.

'Nick her,' Wise said to Panhandle.

Panhandle started to read the caution to Nina, who sat looking at Fitz throughout it. In the end, he turned his back. Those eyes . . . crazy for him. It made him sick to his stomach to think of it. When it was over, she let

204

Panhandle lead her downstairs, though Wise tagged along next to them.

Fitz followed them. Skelton was coming up the stairs as they went down. Wise paused. Yellow light from a low-wattage bulb cast gloomy shadows over all of them.

'Search this lot,' Wise said. 'Shops, the lot.'

'I've seen her,' Skelton said. 'She works at the university. Drives a red Escort van.'

Jesus, Fitz thought. Works at . . . Janice, that was her name. Irene's lab technician, there under his nose all the time.

'You've interviewed her?' Wise demanded.

'The wheelbase matched, but the tyres didn't,' Skelton said.

Temple came up the stairs to join them.

'You'd better be right.' Wise jabbed a finger at Skelton. Skelton nodded. If the tyres match the pattern from the ones at the last murder, I'm going to tear his throat out, Fitz thought. He could have saved Mark. He could have . . . but that wasn't important.

'There's some garages down the back,' Temple said.

'Well go and open them up,' Wise yelled. 'Go on,' he said to Skelton. 'Don't wait for permission – just find that bloody van.'

Wise hurried on downstairs. Fitz matched him pace for pace. 'I know who she is,' he said.

'Go on then,' Wise said.

'Her name's Janice,' Fitz said. 'She's Irene Jackson's lab technician.' If he rubs my face in the fact that I was wrong – that she's not a student, let alone a mature one – I'm going to deck him.

But all Wise said was, 'Good. That saves us some
time. Want me to get Professor Jackson down here?'

They were at the car. Janice had already been taken
away. As they got in, Fitz said, 'Can't hurt.' Anything
that might help. Anything . . .

SEVENTEEN

'I love you, I love you, I love you,' Fitz said. He paced up and down in front of Janice as Wise looked on. The interview room was dimly lit, intimate, as he'd requested it. 'I love you, I love you, I love you . . .' He stopped in front of her and leaned across the table at her. She smiled slightly. He wondered if she realised how pretty she was – and whatever he thought of her, she was pretty – but he rather thought not. Her eyes were wide, large pupilled. That was the light, but they would have looked like that anyway: it was a sign of sexual desire. 'I love you, I love you,' he repeated. She was rapt, intent on his every word, as if she'd been waiting all her life to hear them. Maybe she had. 'No,' he sighed. 'It isn't working, is it?' he said, though he knew for her it was. He pulled back and sat down opposite her. 'I can make you smile –' though now the smile had died, 'but you don't believe it.' He made sure his posture mirrored hers, hands stretched out in front of him, tips of the fingers close together. Subconsciously, she would register it. Subconsciously, she would believe him to be on her side. 'I *understand* you. That's far more rewarding, isn't it?' She was still staring at him. For now, it didn't much matter what he said. He had to gain her trust, though he'd rather have cozied up to a black-widow spider. 'Love comes and goes, but i[...] someone *understands* you, no one can take that away.[...] She wanted that. Her desperation was written on he[r] face. 'Where's Mark?' he asked quietly, hoping the *no[n] sequitur* would surprise her into answering.

She looked taken aback, as if he'd asked her if she'[d] like to fly to the moon. But that wasn't an answer, an[d] he realised he wasn't going to get one.

He pulled some photographs out of the folder Wis[e] had given him. 'He's only guilty of one of their crimes,['] he said as he took the picture of the old man she'[d] mown down and put it aside. He put the picture o[f] Steven Lowry in front of her – blond, blue-eyed, grin[-] ning with a cheerful disregard for his own mortality[.] 'Bright, happy, sexually indiscriminate young men,' h[e] said, and put the picture of John Branaghan next to it. I[n] all important respects they were the same. 'Mark's no[t] that bright,' he said, though he wasn't really so sure o[f] that – when Mark wanted to be, he was as bright as the next lad: he'd proved that when he helped Fitz under[-] stand the physics underlying Kenneth Trant's weird view of cosmology. Calling him stupid now was like [a] betrayal. Yet it was necessary. If Fitz could get Janice t[o] be even a bit sympathetic to Mark – better, if he coul[d] get her to identify with him – she might not want to kil[l] him. 'And he's not very happy at the moment,' he wen[t] on quickly, not allowing himself to dwell on that word[,] *kill*. Again, he tried a *non sequitur*. 'Did he make love to you?'

'No.'

'Did you ask him to?'

She didn't answer, but her face said it all: she had[.]

208

and she took the rejection as a personal slur.

'I'm sure normally he wouldn't let you down and I apologise on his behalf,' he said. He had all her attention now. He was letting her into secrets, making her part of his circle of friends, his family, even. How she must crave that. It didn't matter how many friends of her own she had, she'd always feel alone, always be the outsider. The low self-esteem would do that to her. How, she would spend her lonely nights wondering, how could anyone want to be friends with her? And if they did, there must be something wrong with them, because anyone who wasn't a loser would reject her. So she'd fixed on the unobtainable, which could never reject her. Only now the unobtainable was sitting right opposite her. In her mind, he was the Ideal. What greater validation could there be, than for him to bring her into his life? 'But Mark's very depressed at the moment,' Fitz said, keeping his voice low. 'I feel very privileged at the moment because I know something about him his mother doesn't.' Janice leaned forward slightly. Now she was going to know it too. Fitz was going to make her feel more important than Judith. She'd lived for this moment, this validation. He could see it in her eyes. With luck, she'd also feel sorry for Mark. Put the two together and she might just tell him . . . 'A few months back Mark got his girlfriend pregnant – Debbie's her name.' Judith would be watching on the monitor in the interview room. Fitz could only imagine the effect this would have on her. But that was just tough. All that mattered was finding him. Finding his boy. 'He's depressed because she lost the baby and he's depressed because Debbie gave

209

him the big kiss-off.' Janice was all sympathy now. Good. 'So you can appreciate, he's not himself.' She nodded. Something about her expression just wasn't right, though. 'So I'd prefer he didn't suffer any more,' Fitz said. He could barely say the words. He had to hope it was real, that sympathy. 'So I'd like you to tell me where he is please, Janice.' And he had it then – her expression was that of the professional counsellor, offering him compassion, telling him she understood how he felt. God knows he'd probably worn that same expression himself a thousand times. Maybe she thought she was letting him know what a kind person she was, what a caring individual. How alike they were, both enabling other people to come to terms with their grief. Maybe she thought that would win him over to her.

Well, she could forget that. He stared at her, holding her gaze, hoping she would realise that the only way she could win anything from him was to stop this *now*.

But she was wise to that. She looked away.

He pulled out more pictures of John Branaghan and shoved them across the table at her, so they slid under her clasped hands. She looked down at them almost involuntarily: forensic photographs. Branaghan's body, fish-belly white against the dark mud. His face, with the lips skinned back in that screaming death-smile. The wrists, charred black from the electricity that had surged through them.

For a moment, he thought she'd made the connection, and realised that she had done this. Not someone else who sometimes used her body for its own purposes, but she, herself, Janice.

'We didn't come here to talk about *Mark*!' she snarled.

And then he couldn't do it any more. 'If that's the way my boy ends up, I'll see you dead, you murdering bitch,' he screamed at her.

He hauled himself up out of his chair and stalked out of the room, through the incident room and to his filing cabinet where he kept the Scotch. They were all watching him – Judith, Panhandle, uniforms and all. Well, let them watch. He wrenched the top off the Scotch and took a couple of big gulps of the stuff. It burned when it hit, and he had to concentrate to stop himself gagging on it.

More, he thought. But he couldn't let himself have more. He had to keep his wits about him if he were going to beat the bitch.

She'd looked hurt when he'd shouted at her. Good. It wasn't half the way she'd look by the time he'd finished with her.

The fat policeman was standing far too close to her and yammering in Janice's ear. 'You give us Mark and we'll do a deal.'

'Shut up.' Didn't he realise how unimportant he was? Fitz wasn't in the room. All she wanted to do was to get through the minutes until he came back and the world became real again.

'You'll come out better in court,' he said.

She stared at the rectangles of light pearling through the textured glass in the door. 'Shut up.'

'If you don't help yourself, you'll never see daylight again, love.'

'Shut up,' she snarled.

He backed away. That was better.

A shadowy figure appeared at the door, and rapped loudly. 'Come in,' Wise said. He almost sounded relieved. Good. Let them be scared of her. That just meant they'd have to send Fitz back in.

Penhaligon opened the door. She raised her eyebrows at Wise, who hurried to join her.

'They've found the van,' she said. 'It was empty.'

Of course it was, Janice thought. They were bloody fools to have expected him to be in it.

Wise glared at her for a second, then went out. Penhaligon came in, but she didn't make the mistake of trying to talk to Janice. She just found a seat in the corner and sat down. The uniformed officer who'd been in the room the whole time started to close the door, but Fitz pushed it open.

He came in. It was as if all the lights in the room had suddenly been turned on. How could anyone not love him? Janice sat up a bit straighter.

What was he going to say to her? What secrets would he reveal this time?

He sat down. 'Did you know there were only nine years between Edison discovering how to make the light bulb and the invention of the electric chair?' he asked conversationally. Janice didn't understand why he wanted to talk about that, but she was willing to listen, to follow his logic. If nothing else, she loved the sound of his voice – that Scottish burr, so imprecise yet framing ideas of such precision. He didn't let her down. 'Don't you think that's a statement on eternity?' he asked.

She wanted to say yes, to engage him in a philosophical discussion. She'd dreamt of that, of giving him the intellectual stimulation that Judith could never provide: they'd split a bottle of wine by candlelight and discuss Nietzsche and Mill and Russell, all as a preliminary to making love, of course ... She would have said that, but Fitz was carrying on, and she wanted to follow his argument.

'A few thousand years, waiting for light in the dark depths of winter, and it's transformed into an instrument of destruction,' he said. She nodded to show she understood. 'You know why they chose the chair?' Of course she did. It was just general knowledge. She hoped Fitz wasn't going to do what the others did, and assume she was thick. 'Because it's clean, fast and painless?' She nodded again, sure she had read that somewhere. Fitz's face transformed itself into a sneer. 'They lied,' he said. Janice felt her eyes go wide with shock. Surely he hadn't said all that just to trap her? He was her Fitz. He wouldn't do that to her. 'First belt, the body goes rigid, the eyeballs explode, they urinate,' he said. His jaw clenched and she knew he was thinking of Steven, of John, of Mark. If only he'd paid attention to me earlier, she thought; then he wouldn't have to be going through this now. 'Is that love?' he asked her. She shrugged. She didn't know. She'd never felt that she knew what love was. 'Fifteen, twenty minutes, they're frying like fish,' he said. Yes, she thought, she remembered that, the acrid smell of it, like chops burning under a hot grill. And the smell of shit everywhere. She still wasn't sure she'd got it out of the sheets. 'Your bills are going through the roof and these bastards still aren't dead.'

He'd lain there on the bed, John had – back arched, mouth pulled back into a scream the masking tape wouldn't release, chest trying to move and trying to move and trying to move until at last she'd turned the electricity off and he'd fallen in on himself like a puppet with the strings cut, only the smile remaining and his blind eyes staring up at her.

Well, it was his own fault. The cocky bastard shouldn't have said he was leaving her. Fitz should have spoken to her properly that day in the pub. And in any case she didn't have to think about it. Didn't have to think about the timer counting down, waiting to send the current surging through Mark.

'It must have come as a surprise that they don't die pleasantly at all?' She looked away from him. He did think she was stupid. He threw a sheaf of papers on to the table in front of her. Her own picture stared up at her from the photo attached to her personnel file. Her CV was under it. 'Course not,' Fitz said. 'HND Electronics, Stoke. You know better than most of us that it's the single, most barbaric method of execution imaginable. So why'd you choose it, Janice?' She wouldn't look at him. She didn't have to. He couldn't make her. Why wouldn't he admit his part of the guilt? That if he'd only cared about her, she wouldn't have had to do it? 'I'll tell you why,' he said. Yes, she thought. Tell me Fitz. Explain it to me, because now you've asked me I'm not sure I know. She remembered thinking about it, remembered making the logical connections that made it seem the most sensible thing to do; but she couldn't put them back together. 'It gave you time,' he said, 'and time over a dying man is the ultimate power. They had to listen to you, didn't they, Janice? With the electricity screaming through them, forcing their mouths into that

214

dying, wordless, soundless scream.' Yes, she thought. Yes. 'They couldn't answer you back then, could they? So what was it you wanted to say without contradiction, fixing their smiles so they couldn't look appalled by your confessions?' He wasn't smiling at her. She wanted to make him smile. 'Speak to me.'

She stared at him. What could he possibly think she had to confess to them? To him? Anything she said might drive him away, so she said nothing.

'Surely you've got something to say about taking a psychology degree?'

'No,' Janice said. He was being ridiculous. What could she possibly have had to say to a pair of mouthy gobshite kids about their puerile studies?

'Possibly that you didn't get one?' he demanded. He was so intense. She loved that about him. 'Booted off the course after six terms because you couldn't hack it.'

'My dad died –' It was the first thing that came into her head.

'You *failed*,' Fitz contradicted her. 'But that's OK, we've all done it.'

He was giving her a way out, but she knew what lay down that road: listen to him, agree with him, and the first thing that happened would be that she'd admitted everything; the second would be that she'd told him where Mark was; and after that there'd be no need for him to speak to her, no need for him to sit opposite her with those huge brown eyes watching every move she made, seeing right into her soul. 'My father died,' she insisted. The words sounded right. They sounded true. Maybe they had their own kind of truth.

Fitz would understand that.

Perhaps he did. He didn't challenge her any more. Not that that brought her much relief. 'You went back a a lab technician,' he said. 'Surrounded yourself with al these young, promising, bright, sexy people. Why dic you put yourself through that amount of pain?' I only wanted to be like them, Janice thought. I just wanted tc share in it, that's all. 'To prove that even though you couldn't get a degree, you could get a job on the staff. Swan around in a lab coat with your name tag. At least the first years would look up to you?'

There was contempt in his eyes. Of course there was. He was a psychologist. She'd failed to become one. How could he respect someone who was less than he was? Janice swallowed. She would have to prove to him that she could have done it. If they'd given her a chance, if things hadn't gone wrong. She could have been the equal of Steven Lowry or John Branaghan.

He was taking her apart, analysing everything she was, everything she'd done, everything she'd hoped to be. The only way to prove herself a fit companion was to do the same to him.

'May 1990, you gave a lecture,' she said. 'It was like, half-ten, and you were still pissed from the night before. The board outside said PSYCHOLOGY OF FAMILY STRUC-TURE, DR EDWARD FITZGERALD. You acted out a row you'd had with your wife that morning.' She smiled at the memory of it, felt herself relax into that memory of a happier time. It had been magical, watching him. 'You stood to the left when you were playing her –' she moved to illustrate her point, 'to the right as yourself . . .' She had him now: in her mind, giving that lecture that had stunned her so; in the real world, watching her,

216

watching her, wanting to know what she would say next. 'You'd just moved to a big house and she'd got a loan on a car and you'd been into the office – that morning – and packed your job in. You were going to write a book and she said you weren't capable of writing your own name.' Now he was the one who couldn't meet her gaze. She hated hurting him, hated herself for doing it to him. But it was necessary. She had to make him understand that she understood him, that she was fit to be with him. He stared at his hands, and she had to hold herself back from curling her fingers round his. There would be time for that later. All the time in the world, once this awful night was over. 'And all the students were laughing . . .' He was embarrassed now, and her heart went out to him. But that was all right. She would make it be all right. 'And I just remember sitting at the back and thinking, oh God, he's completely trapped.' She put everything she had into that. He had to understand that she was on his side, that of all the people in the world, she understood the horror that had been his life till now. 'He's got kids he never wanted in a house his mother-in-law persuaded them to buy and if they just listened to him for two minutes they'd know he's talking *sense*.' She had him now. She could see it in his eyes, that terrible, unanswered need for love. She could answer it. She would, if he would only let her. 'I went back to my room and cried.' She'd embarrassed him. She wished there was some other way; but what he needed was for her to understand him: he'd said it himself – what greater love could there be than to understand someone. And once she'd shown him the truth of his situation, then he would be free to admit the love that he was repressing at the moment. And so, painful as it was for both of them, she went on. 'And I'm back, like *five years* later and you're still doing the rounds and nothing's changed. That's failure.'

There, she thought. Her analysis was complete and inarguable. He'd have to admit now that she was at least his equal, and that, if either of them needed to make changes to their lives, it wasn't her, it was him.

But he came back immediately. 'No Janice. That's *family*. All that squealing, all that anguish. That's like cats pissing up door-frames . . . Marking territory. When you *belong* to someone, you constantly test the barriers.' It was rubbish. Her Fitz, talking rubbish to try and protect himself from the knowledge that his marriage was a sham. 'That's what families do when they love each other, when they belong to each other, Janice,' he said. But it was nonsense. She knew what families were: they were quiet places where you swallowed your pride, backed down when trouble loomed, sidestepped arguments. How could anyone live their lives rowing all the time? 'That's *normal*,' he said.

He reached into his inside pocket. The light glinted on his wedding ring. She'd have to persuade him to take that off. When he was ready. She didn't want to make him feel rushed.

He pulled out his wallet and started going through it. She remembered him buying it from Marriotts, in the town. She'd sat and watched him from her van. Katie had been with him. The wallet had been her birthday present to him. Janice did hope he wasn't going to miss the girl too much. Well, he could always visit her. Every other weekend. That was the usual thing, wasn't it?

'You killed these men because you were jealous of their futures, but they had none.' He put a picture down on the table. Mark, much younger, holding a football and wearing a team strip. His hair was cut short. It didn't suit him very well, Janice thought. 'Another jealous woman beat you to it – Thatcher. She crushed a whole generation and made you look like a bloody amateur.'

Mark was nice-looking, Janice thought. She reached for the picture. Fitz batted her hand away. '*Don't* touch it,' he said. And then Janice knew what the problem was. He was jealous of his own son. Of course he was – Mark was younger than he was, with his whole life ahead of him and, he was far more conventionally good-looking. And Janice had almost gone to bed with him. Fitz might not be ready to admit it, but his subconscious certainly knew that he was in love with her. Of course he was jealous of Mark. Why else would he have demanded to know whether they had made love? Why else would he be making their time together revolve round him, instead of working out how they could be together? He stared levelly at her, and she met his gaze. 'He waited nineteen years for his first job. You've seen where he ended up – shovelling shit into take-away cartons for two quid an hour. So if you take him away, maybe the world won't miss him.' Oh God, he was nearly crying. How could she not love a man who wasn't ashamed to cry. 'I will,' he said. 'Right now, I'd *die* for him. I'd *die* for my family, and that's where you and I are completely different.'

We're not, she thought. We're the same. It's just that I recognise what I am, and you can't see what you are. But I can help you. I will . . .

219

The door opened behind him. 'Fitz?' Wise said from the doorway.

Fitz picked the photograph of Mark up with infinite tenderness. Then he got up and started to go out. Penhaligon followed him. Janice couldn't let him leave her. Not without one more attempt at making him see sense.

'So how come you were screwing her?' she asked as they got to the door. Penhaligon whirled round. She looked appalled. That was good. Janice had wanted to see that expression for a long time. Fitz turned more slowly. He looked at the floor and rubbed his chin. Janice smiled. There was no letting him off the hook now. That wouldn't be a kindness. He had to be brought to seeing the truth behind his self-deceptions. 'If you'd live and die for your family, how come you were screwing her?' She had the tone exactly right, just like the one the counsellors at college had used in their practise sessions.

Fitz looked at her, then at the floor. The one place he wouldn't look was at Penhaligon. That was good. Janice had to drive a wedge between them, make him see how false his dependence on her was. 'Every cripple has his own way of walking,' he said at last.

Penhaligon didn't like that. Janice smiled. There'd be no going back for them now.

'You see, that's when I knew,' Janice said. It was time to lay it out in front of him, to unravel the secret of his sadness for him, so he could move beyond it. 'That was your cry for help. When I followed you home and she didn't come out till morning – but that wasn't real. You were desperate to change your life but you didn't have he guts to just tell your wife and leave her.' His expression changed as he acknowledged the truth of what she was saying. The blood pounded in her ears. This was it, the single moment the rest had been made for. She leaned forward eagerly, feeling herself flushing with excitement. 'I understand that.' It was obvious from his expression that he knew. 'It's difficult to leave your wife when you haven't met the right person.' He was looking at her now with an expression she'd never seen before, and she knew she'd won. She stood up. Licked her lips. She'd thought she would be nervous, but she wasn't. She felt calm and peaceful. She'd come home. 'I'm offering you a life, Fitz.' And still he looked at her. 'I love you.' He started to walk towards her, then stopped. 'I'm offering you a future,' she said tenderly.

'You have killed and I have not,' he said, and she saw with horror that his expression was hard with hatred. 'You definitely don't have a future.'

But he was wrong. He had to be wrong. 'If you bury your son tomorrow, and I go to prison, you'll have to think of me every day for the rest of your life.' She thought about it – him, waking up beside Judith and thinking of her; making love to Penhaligon, and thinking of her; lecturing on forensic psychology, and thinking of her. It was enough. It was more than enough, more than she had ever dreamed she could have from anyone. To be at the centre of his life, the pivot on which all else turned. *That's* a future,' she said.

She smiled.

Judith watched as Fitz came out of the interview room. The things that girl had said, finding out about Mark getting some girl she'd never even *met* pregnant, Fitz's adultery with the stick insect laid out for all to see – she had to talk to him. She didn't mind. She told herself she didn't mind, not if it meant they were closer to finding Mark.

But Fitz was busy with Wise. 'I don't want you going back in there,' the DCI said.

'What?' Fitz muttered.

They can't do this, Judith thought, looking at her husband. He's the only one who stands a chance. Quite apart from anything else, he's the only one who's got any leverage with that bloody bitch.

'You're not up to it,' Wise said.

'What!' Fitz bellowed, and for once Judith agreed with him. He'd seemed to be doing quite well. As well as could be expected, if you didn't count finding out where Mark was.

Which was the only thing that really mattered.

Judith felt the tears begin to prick at her eyes again. Penhaligon was watching. I'm not crying, not with her here, Judith thought. Being comforted by the stick insect was the last thing she could stand.

'We've got her sister in Number Two,' Wise said.

Fitz nodded. 'Irene?'

Judith stared wonderingly at him. How could he be so calm, so controlled?

'Wasn't in. Don't know where she is,' Wise said.

'OK,' Fitz said. 'And the father?'

'Lives in Prestwich. He's being fetched.'

Fitz chewed his lip. 'Not worth waiting for. Let's go.'

He walked straight past Judith. She reached for him,

ut he ignored her. Penhaligon was following him, but he stopped to get something from a filing cabinet, and Judith suddenly realised that they weren't going to leave her alone. Maybe they thought she'd try to kill the girl.

They might have a point.

She stared at Penhaligon's bony back, the long bush of red hair tied neatly into a pony tail. 'Well, that makes three of us now,' she said at last. Penhaligon turned, holding a file. 'Three dogs, chasing the same bone,' Judith explained. Penhaligon smiled, as if they were colluding in a practical joke. Judith wanted to scrub it off her face. She isn't even pretty, she thought contemptuously, though she knew a lot of men would disagree. 'Did you believe him when he said he loved *you*?' she asked.

Penhaligon stared at her, clearly weighing her words. She didn't look the least bit amused now. 'No,' she said after a while. She said it as if it were a gift. Or maybe it was for Fitz.

'Why not?' Judith asked. She thought, keep this up, keep asking questions, and she'll have to say something hurtful. Yet she couldn't stop herself. Wouldn't have taken the words back if she could.

'He always went back to you,' Penhaligon said. She laughed ruefully, but her fingers, holding the folder, were white at the knuckles; and this time Judith was in no doubt that Penhaligon's words were a gift for Judith, and Judith alone. She started to walk away. The overhead lights struck copper from her red hair. She got to the door and hesitated, then turned. 'I've handed my resignation in,' she said. 'I leave in six months' time.'

She paused, it seemed to Judith for ever. 'If that helps.'

And that was the second thing she'd given Judith.

Nina stared down at the terrible photographs laid out before her on the table. Dead men – boys, really – stared up at her. Charred flesh. Mouths blue-white with lack of blood. Empty eye-sockets accusing her.

When she couldn't stand it any more, she looked at the two men opposite her. They were both big men. The one with the beard and glasses was a policeman. Detective Chief Inspector Wise, in charge of the investigation. The other one was Fitz, a psychologist. How often had she joked to Louise and Colin that Janice needed to see a shrink? I didn't mean it, she thought. I never meant it, not really. But she had, and she knew it.

She swallowed hard. 'Janice isn't a murderer,' she whispered. 'I want to get her a lawyer,' she said.

'She doesn't want a lawyer,' Wise said. He jerked his head at the photographs. 'Just answer the questions.'

Anyone would have thought she was the one they were accusing.

'Janice isn't the youngest, then?' Fitz asked. He tapped ash from his cigarette into a glass ashtray. Blue smoke plumed upwards.

Nina shook her head. 'Louise. Twenty-two.' She licked her lips. It was all very well answering their questions, but what about Janice? 'Look, I want to see her,' she said. 'I want to talk to her. Where is she?'

'What did your father do?'

The question took her by surprise. She'd been saying something. All Nina's worry, and Janice had been telling her tales again. 'I beg your pardon?' she said.

'What did your father do?' Fitz repeated.

They knew. They *knew*. 'Nothing,' she said. 'He did othing ...' She felt her heart hammering at her ribs. Ier mouth was dry. 'If she's telling you that and she's laming Dad for –' she glanced at the pictures, and then way, before she had to think about them '– *this*, well, he's talking crap.' They were staring at her. 'She's lways said it, she's *always* pretended. She's built her vhole fucking life around fantasies.' She leaned forvard. They were still staring at her, like she was an xhibit in a zoo or something. 'But I swear, he did *othing*,' she screamed.

There was a pause, in which Nina could hear nothing ut the sound of her own breathing.

'I meant as an occupation,' Fitz said mildly.

She'd told them. She'd given it away. She'd promsed ... 'He was –' she said, and couldn't speak for ears. She tried again. 'He was a butcher.'

And then the tears came, and all she could do was :over her face with her hands and pretend that no one :ould see her.

He had her now, had the key that would enable him to anlock the secret of Janice Cochrane.

'Why'd you call yourself Nina?' he asked her.

Janice made a theatrical show of thinking about it. 'First name that came into my head,' she said.

'I can understand why you'd want to choose it,' Fitz said. 'Nina. Much prettier name than Janice.' He tapped ash from his cigarette into a half-empty plastic coffee cup, suddenly aware that it was a disgusting thing to do, and that Panhandle was sitting quietly in the corner, watching everything that went on. There'd been a time when a large part of his purpose in one of these interviews was to impress her: but that was when he was talking to ordinary rapists, average killers, not the only person who could tell him how to save his son's life.

'It's also your sister's name.'

Janice's fingers flexed against the Formica table-top. 'Who've you been talking to?' she demanded.

'Got any other siblings?'

'No,' she snapped back. Just for a second she couldn't look him in the eye.

'Liar.' He stared at her for a moment. She stared back at him, and again her face held that expression it had had in her flat: not collusion, he thought, not an in joke – no, that was the expression of a naughty child waiting to be punished. The father was the key. Sex and death would get you a long way, but if they failed then dragging the parents in would generally take you further.

'When did your father die?'

Janice blinked slowly. 'Nineteen ninety-one,' she said uncertainly.

'Month?'

'July,' she said without hesitation.

And here's one I prepared earlier, Fitz thought. 'Time of day?' he asked, taking his cigarette out of his mouth.

'I don't know what time of day,' she snarled.

'You're a bloody liar,' Fitz said. He drowned the dog-end in the coffee. 'If your father was dead, you'd be blaming yourself. Every girl needs her dad.' He stared at the table, thinking of Katie, sitting at home with a neighbour to look after her and no idea what was going on. It came into his mind, quite unbidden, that for her

226

ke, if no other, he would have to try and save his
arriage. But that was a problem for another day. First
 had to save his son. 'The question is, how much does
 father need his daughter.' That got her. *Finally*, he
 ought, as he stared back at her horror-struck face.
 ou were abused, weren't you,' he murmured.

'No!' The denial was absolute. Shit, Fitz thought. Of
 urse she'd deny it. They always did. How long had he
 t to break her down? Mark might already be dead, of
 course, in which case he had all the time in the
 orld . . . but Fitz didn't think so. He didn't dare.

It was a thing about hostages: once they were dead,
 e hostage-taker had no more power over those she
 as negotiating with. Janice wanted Fitz's attention; if
 ark were dead, he'd have no reason to talk to her. He
 d to hope that she'd simply locked him up some-
 here, that sooner or later she'd start using that as bait
 keep Fitz talking.

If he couldn't break her, he'd have to make a show of
 lling them that he believed Mark was already dead, to
 ck her up and throw away the key. But he couldn't
 ar to say the words, couldn't bear the effect it would
 ve on Judith. Besides, it was a bluff he could only try
 ce, and at the moment he thought Janice was still
 rong enough to call it.

So: 'You are pursuing a father who doubles as a lover,
 father figure who can do better than the first one. You
 e in a flat –'

'I was not abused,' Janice cut in. She seemed almost
 risive.

Fitz filed that piece of information for later. Some-
 ing else about her reaction? Not studied, he thought.

227

For once she's not lying. Or doesn't think she is. Again it was a typical reaction '– which looks like Barbie playpen,' he said without stopping.

'I was not abused.' She was furious, but almost i tears around her anger. Good. It was a defensive reac tion, but those defences would be brittle. When the broke, she would snap into a million pieces.

'You could have got that pain recognised anywhere he said. 'It's every therapist's bloody mortgage, fc God's sake.'

'I was not abused.'

'Is that why you're punishing Mark?'

She glared at him. 'The one thing you do right an you're screwing it up.' Her lips twisted into a sneer tha made her pretty face ugly. 'You're going backwards. was not abused.' There was no blinking now, no failu to meet his eyes.

And then she was almost in tears. Struggling wit them. She isn't lying he thought. If I can't get her admit to it, I've failed. Failed her, failed myself, faile Mark.

Failed Mark.

This was what she'd come here for. This was wha she'd killed two men for – three, counting the incider tal. This was why she might – please God, not, bu might – have killed Mark. Free-floating anxiety woul have brought her down, caused depression in her all he life, made her – what had Nina said? – made her buil her life round fantasies. But such fantasies. So man victims repressed the memories, invented remembere childhoods of absolute perfection. But what had Janic done? Said that Nina was abused. Told Nina's husban at their father had abused Nina. Whatever Janice was pressing, it wasn't a memory of abuse.

He knew it. He felt the jolt go through him, that perfect moment for which he lived, that instant of knowing, and knowing he was right, and knowing that most nobody else on the face of the planet could have worked it out.

'*You* weren't,' he whispered. Janice's head came up. There was recognition in her eyes. She gazed at him intently, waiting for him to say it and set her free. 'You weren't. Nina was. Louise was. But *you weren't*.'

He stared at her, long and hard. She hadn't repressed the thought. She'd never forgotten what had happened to her sisters, or that it hadn't happened to her. She didn't need him to help her remember. Perhaps she thought she'd come through it all right. That she was normal. But she'd never managed to form a lasting relationship – Nina had laughed at the idea of Janice having a boyfriend. And then she saw Fitz and . . . what? Saw an old fat clever guy with a dysfunctional family? Saw someone so obviously screwed-up that she thought he'd never reject her? Maybe. But he'd said himself that she didn't want love, she wanted under-standing.

And then he had it. She wanted to know why – why she'd been rejected by her father. Ironically, she wanted to know why she'd been allowed to have the so-called normal childhood her sisters had surely craved.

'Nina you could rationalise,' he said. 'Her card was marked even before you were of age.' Janice was staring at him intently, as if she were willing him on, willing him to understand her. 'But then he started picking Louise, and that made you piggy in the middle. The one who got nothing unless it had the ribbons o it?' he asked. 'How awful,' he whispered, as if genuinely appalled him, this spectre of a childhood warped by the fact of its normality. 'Not pretty enoug not clever enough.'

'I am,' she wailed.

'– too old and not old enough,' he went on relen lessly. He was enjoying himself, he realised. Enjoy ing the hunt, the adrenalin burst pumping throug his arteries, letting him know he was alive. And, h realised, he hadn't thought about Mark at all in at lea five minutes. If he'd had time, he'd have hated himse for it. As it was, all he could do was go on. 'And you'v been wondering all your life what you did wrong.'

He was hurting her. Cutting to the heart of all h fantasies, all the lies that were the life she'd built f herself, all the delusions that protected her from th awful knowledge that she wasn't even good enough f her father, let alone anyone else. It was no wonder she' tried to tell Nina's new husband about what had ha pened. How could she bear to realise that Nina wasn only good enough for her father, she was good enoug for other men, too?

'You'd better shut your mouth,' she said.

And that, Fitz thought, was her other defenc mechanism: don't speak, don't let others speak, don listen if they do.

'Why?' he asked gently. 'That's what you came to m for, isn't it?' He went on quickly, without giving he time to disagree. 'But if I give you what you really wan if I meet the challenge, if I really, really understand yo

at's the end of the affair – yes?' And, he thought, you
ay not know it yet, but then you will tell me where
ark is . . . you murdering bitch. He suppressed the
ithet. To do what must be done, he had to get inside
r head, sympathise with her – almost become her.

Janice nodded quickly, barely taking her eyes off him
r a second.

'Nina, Louise – you knew it caused them pain, you
ew it made them cry.' He held himself very still.
: didn't want anything to distract her, to break the
armed web of words he was spinning around her. 'But
least they were getting something from their father.'

'Yes,' she murmured so quietly he had to strain to
ar.

'Their secret. All of them.'

She nodded, a tiny, almost imperceptible movement.
at was good. She was mirroring his body language
w. It meant the rapport was building between them.

'Your mother knew?' Again the nod, but this time an
en smaller movement of her head. She was regress-
g, becoming the shy, inhibited child she'd learned to
de as she grew up and grew away from her family. 'A
rce rejection,' Fitz said. 'A tiny girl wanting the same
tention.' He stood up and walked round behind her.
ie didn't move, didn't try to keep watching him. That
orried him for a moment, until he realised that she was
st in memories, becoming the small damaged child
at she once had been. 'Trying to smile, begging the
iestions,' he said.

'Yes.'

He moved in behind her, bent low and whispered in
r ear. 'There were no rows in your house, because

231

nobody wanted to take the lid off.' He could hear h
breathing, deep and slow, almost like a hypnosis su
ject. 'You were the only one screaming, Janice,'
said, then changed his tone to one of severity. Scho
masterish. Fatherly. 'Naughty girl, asking too ma
questions.'

He moved away, over to the cassette deck he'd h
placed in the room earlier, waiting for the right momen

'They just kept lying, but I *knew*,' Janice said. S
sounded near to tears again.

Oh, she'd cry all right, by the time he'd finished wi
her.

He took a long, long drag on his cigarette, then hit t
play button. The first few bars of the Dusty Springfie
number filled the little interview room. Janice stiffene

'This isn't your song, is it?' he asked. She did
answer. He hadn't expected her to. 'You're far t
young.' But she was lost in the music. 'Did your fath
play this?'

'They played it for him on his fortieth,' she said. Th
surprised Fitz. He'd been sure she was going to say h
father had played it all the time – perhaps as a signal
wanted Louise or Nina, perhaps to drown out t
sounds of illicit sex. But then she went on, in th
dreamy voice, 'He kept staring at me. He walked acro
and asked me to dance. Nina was watching. Louise w
watching. I couldn't see Mum, but I knew she w
watching.' She sounded so proud, so desperately prou
that for a moment Fitz felt genuinely sorry for her. 'H
kissed me there,' she said, and laid her fingers on th
side of her mouth. 'He was looking at me, and I start
shaking.' Her expression changed, hardened, as sh

232

nembered. 'He just laughed and sat back down.'

That was it, Fitz thought: that was the moment when
e, however distorted, curdled and turned to hatred.
e wouldn't realise that, of course, but it had. That was
y she used the Dusty Springfield song, and not one
m her childhood; and that was why, when she finally
:ided to love someone else, it had taken the form
obsession, stalking and, finally, murder. What else
uld you do to someone you love but humiliate them
d hurt them?

She started to play with her hair, first winding it
nd her fingers like a child, and then brushing it back
t of her face. Fitz thought perhaps her father had done
it. Maybe when he went up to say goodnight to her.
'd have done it to Louise and Nina too, but in their
se it would have been the prelude to something else,
me other, much more intense touching; and he would
ve ignored the fact that when he touched their hair,
y flinched away from him. But it was as much
ching as he ever did to Janice, yearn for more
wever much she might.

She was so locked in the past ... wherever she
d Mark, it would be a place she knew. Somewhere
sonant with memories of happiness thwarted, old
miliations, ancient pain. How else to exorcise those
emories but by handing the agony on to other vic-
ns? But he couldn't ask her outright. She'd know then
at all his sympathy was manufactured, aimed only at
tting her to tell him where Mark was. He didn't think
e was ready to do that yet, and if he lost her now it
uld take him hours to get her back to this point.

'Did your father slaughter his own meat, Janice?' he

asked. She nodded, still playing with her hair. 'That w
a built-up area, he wouldn't leave them squealing in t
yard.'

'He electrocuted them,' she said. 'In the head.' S
laid her two fingers against her temple as gently as s
had when she demonstrated her father's kiss.

'In the shop?'

'When he'd closed for the day, Mum used to take r
out for walks on the embankment.'

'Dunston Embankment?' Fitz looked past Janice,
Panhandle. She'd picked it up all right. Sharp as knive
Panhandle.

Janice barely nodded. Her fingers stopped weavin
themselves through her hair. She was deep in it no
deep in the memory of that time she'd never been ab
to leave, never been able to outgrow or move beyond.

'She said he was doing the meat but I knew he w
upstairs with Nina. I could see.' She was soft no
barely recognisable as the screaming harridan who
told him to shut up, shut up, shut up. 'We'd be walkir
and Mum kept talking and talking, but I looked ba
and I could see him at the upstairs window, pullir
down the blinds.' Fitz caught Panhandle's eye agai
and this time she got up and left. Janice didn't ev
notice. She just kept talking. 'And when we came bac
he never had his tie on,' she said. She sounded bew
dered, a small child in a grown-up world she cou
never understand.

Wise pulled the large-scale map off the wall. Pe
haligon shifted things off the desk just in time for hi
to spread it out.

234

They both pored over it. Janice lived now at 16 Brent reet. The father's shop had been next door. 'She could e the shop from the embankment,' he said. He found e place on the map. Penhaligon put her finger on a cond place, very close by. 'That's where the first body rned up,' he acknowledged.

Without waiting to be asked, Penhaligon got on the dio to Temple and Skelton. 'Look next door,' she said. 1 the shop, upstairs.'

'We're there,' Temple said through the static. 'It's icked up.'

Wise grabbed the handset off Penhaligon. 'We've got e van, there's nothing in it. He must be bloody there,' shouted.

'Sir, we've looked everywhere,' Skelton said. Right oody team him and Temple were turning into. Noddy d Big Ears had nothing on them.

Wise swore under his breath. 'I'm coming down yself,' he said.

He ran for the door. Judith was standing in the way, atching him. He brushed past her, and she raced after m. He didn't wait for her.

nice couldn't look at Fitz. How could he love her ow? How could he, when he knew that not even her ther had been able to? So she sat, quiet as a mouse on er chair, staring at the light purling through the win- w.

If it could have been different. If he could have loved er then, maybe Fitz could have loved her now. Maybe meone could.

She didn't know.

He'd said she was plain, wasn't clever. Why did he have to say it? She'd known it anyway.

'But Nina was clever?' he asked. Why wouldn't he leave her alone? She just wanted to be left alone now. To sleep and not wake up.

'Nina was always missing school,' she said. It was true. She was always having stomach cramps. Migraines. She said.

'But she graduated?' Fitz said. 'Degree in art?'

'He paid for extra tuition.' She'd always resented that. When she'd failed her second-year exams, he'd told her she'd have to get on with it. But Nina wouldn't even have made it onto the degree if she hadn't had extra help to sort out her portfolio.

'And Louise?' Fitz asked.

'She's going to bloody medical school!' She couldn't keep the tears at bay. Beautiful Louise. Popular Louise. Did she have to be clever with it? Why couldn't there have been something left over for her? Janice realised that her fingers were knotting in the fabric of her skirt. She tried to stop them, but they just kept on moving, betraying her. He would notice. He noticed everything, knew everything.

'Nina got married last week?' He made it a question. She nodded. Why did they have to talk about her sisters? Why couldn't they talk about each other, about the life of happiness they'd make with each other. Somewhere in her mind, a small voice tried to say that was because they weren't going to have a life together, but she ignored it. But Fitz had asked her something, and she couldn't ignore him. She belonged to him.

'Three days before the first murder. You watched your

ster's crowning glory – fairytale wedding, up the aisle
oking prettier than ever with him on her arm, the
oudest man on earth.' The words were like electric
ocks ripping into her. She swallowed hard, and tasted
ars. 'They made a pact. She wipes the slate clean,
nies her past and he ...' He paused. Don't stop
lking, she thought at him. Don't stop, it's all I've got
 hang on to, your voice, even if you're saying things I
te to hear. But she was crying anyway, and there was
 stopping the tears. 'She's wearing a very expensive
g. Is he helping them financially?' She nodded.
ords were beyond her. 'They got everything they
anted just by smiling back –' Yes, she thought. She'd
ed so hard to learn how to smile the way they did, but
hadn't done any good. '– and keeping their mouths
ut, and you end up in this mess with sweet FA. And
 one can tell you what it is you did wrong.'
 She couldn't bear it. She was pretty. She was. People
id so. Men said so. Only her father had never said it,
 it was lies. People said she was bright, too. She could
ve got her degree, she thought. A bit more work, a bit
ss weeping, she'd have been there. 'No,' she said,
rough her tears. She shook her head, to be sure he
nderstood.
 'I can,' Fitz said. Of course he could, Janice thought.
hat was why she'd chosen him. She had to listen to
m. She took a couple of big, sobbing breaths, and
anaged to calm down enough to hear him. 'I under-
and your father. As a shrink, maybe. But as a man,
 solutely.' Could he, Janice wondered. Maybe he was
st saying it to make her feel better. She loved him,
ter all. She did. She did. His gentle voice went on. 'I

237

can look at you now and see exactly why he reject
you. Why he excluded you. Shall I tell you?'

'Yes.'

'It's clear as day,' Fitz said. 'I can't believe you'
got this far and not understood it.'

She turned to beg him. 'Please, Fitz.'

'A man like that and a girl like you. Is he handsome'

Part of her realised he'd turned something on i
head: he'd said she was ugly and thick; now he w
saying she was beautiful and bright. But she didn't ca
didn't care that he was playing on her emotions, pla
ing with her, getting what he wanted. He had wh
she needed, what she'd always needed. 'Tell me,' sl
wailed, and recognised the sound of herself as a child
that plea, begging Nina to tell her what Daddy h
done, if it was nice, if it was fun.

And like Nina, Fitz wouldn't answer her directl
'You were there, under her nose, the one in the middl
His voice rolled over her, forcing her to remember
those lonely days and lonelier nights, all those walks
the railway track with her mother's voice, talkin
talking, talking, saying anything but the things Jani
needed to hear. 'Pleading for it,' Fitz said. Oh yes, she
done that. Snuggled up to Daddy in her dressing gow
while Nina, jealous as hell – as if she'd needed to be
had pulled her away, told her to leave Daddy alon
leave him alone, Janice. Play with your dollies, Janic
Play with teddy. Don't talk to Daddy, leave him be, he
tired. Oh yes, too tired for Janice, but not for Louis
Not for Nina. 'It's tragic, Janice, that he never cho
you. That he never moved in and made you a part
that family –'

'Tell me,' she begged.

'Where's Mark?' he said gently.

'Please,' she said. She tried to smile at him. You got things if you smiled nicely.

She wasn't smiling right.

'Where's Mark?'

All she could do was cry. He didn't want her to smile. He just wanted her to cry.

'Mark,' he said.

She had to know. It was worth anything to know. 'Next door,' she whispered through the tears. 'Tell them to move the wardrobe.' He stared at her for a heartbeat or two. 'Please,' she said.

But he got up and left the room at a dead run, and then she was alone with the silence that was broken only by the sound of her sobbing.

Mark lay in the darkness, waiting. Only a few of the candles were still burning, but the streetlight outside cast a yellow pallor over everything.

The timer ticked. And ticked. And then paused.

No!

He had time to think that one word. Then the electricity seared through him. He screamed, but the sound was cut off as every muscle in his body went rigid. His body arched back against the bed. His bowels voided.

Then there was nothing but the silence. And pain.

EIGHTEEN

Danny Fitzgerald was drunk.

Very, very drunk. He weaved his way across the casino. He'd never been in one before. It wasn't as noisy as he'd expected. There was a low murmur of voices from each table as he passed, a chink of glasses being filled, the dull clink of chips on baize.

Well, he'd come here to do one thing and one thing only. He didn't understand a lot of the games, but he'd watched enough James Bond movies to know what you did at a roulette table.

He lowered himself into one of the seats very carefully. He didn't want to make a bad impression on the nice young lady. He put his chips down on one of the numbers. All of them. Two thousand pounds worth, same as he'd given Judith.

Around him, others placed their bets. The croupier leaned forward, and he got a flash of cleavage, a whiff of perfume he didn't recognise. 'Last bets,' she said.

She pressed the button, and the wheel spun. The ball flew round, faster and faster till it was nothing but a metallic blur. And slowed, and bounced and stopped. Twenty-four black.

Danny gazed at his chips. Wrong number.

241

He let out a long sigh, then smiled at the croupier. 'I just wanted to know what it felt like to be him,' he said to her, as if it made perfect sense.

She stared at him for a moment, then raked in the house's winnings.

Danny stood up and wandered away. He'd lost, like Eddie lost. Unfortunately, it seemed he'd lost Judith too. Again, like Eddie.

The message from Fitz came through on the radio while they were on the way to Brent Street.

He did it, Judith thought. He did it.

She was out of the car almost before it had stopped. Up the stairs, through the front room, into the bedroom.

Wise and Penhaligon manhandled the wardrobe out of the way. There was a curtain behind it. Wise yanked that aside. He hesitated in the doorway. Beyond it there was a shadowy room. Judith couldn't see in but she could smell the place: burnt wax and urine. She started to push past Wise, but he went in, slowly.

There was a bed. Mark was lying on it, naked, body arched back against the chains that held him. Rigid.

'Mark?' Judith whispered.

'Don't touch him,' Wise snapped. 'Don't touch anything.'

He strode across to the wall and yanked a plug out of an electrical socket. What? Judith wondered, and noticed the trolley of electrical equipment next to the bed, the clamps attached to the iron bedframe.

Mark's body jounced back against the bed. His eyes were closed and his skin was sheened with sweat. He didn't move again.

Please God, Judith thought. Please God, I'll never
k for anything again, only . . .

'He's breathing,' Penhaligon murmured.

Judith looked at her, and realised that was the second
ing Penhaligon had given her that day. First her
sband, now her son.

'Thank you,' she whispered.

the communications room at Anson Road, Fitz took
e call from Wise. He flicked the radio off. For a
oment he stood staring at nothing.

Then a great sob came out of him, and he collapsed
ito a seat, crying and crying and crying, until his
ands were coated in tears and in all the world there was
ly the sound of his weeping.

nice sat waiting for Fitz to come back. She felt empty.
ollow, as if her insides had been ripped out and turned
tears; but she had cried so much there were no tears
ft, so no there was nothing left inside her at all.

She had killed. Steven Lowry. John Branaghan. That
d man. Mark Fitzgerald, maybe. They'd taken her
atch away from her and there wasn't a clock in the
om so she'd lost track of the time.

They would ask her why she'd done it, and she didn't
ave an answer, only that at the time it had seemed the
ost sensible thing in the world. When she'd looked
own on their begging eyes, their silenced mouths, their
ead faces, her rage had drained away, just for a little
hile. But now, nothing.

They would ask, and she wouldn't have an answer
or them.

Are you proud of me now, Dad? she wondered. The thought of him made her smile. The best dad in the world. Why didn't you love me, Dad?

There was no answer, only silence. She couldn't bear that silence, and so she began to sing, '*It's the way you make me feel, Whenever I am close to you . . .*'

The door opened. Fitz came into the room. She couldn't bear to look at him. She wanted to ask if Mar had been alive when they found him, but she couldn' She had done that. She had, no one else.

She'd loved Fitz, and the only way she'd been able t show it was to hurt him.

She wanted to say she was sorry, but she couldn't fin the words. She wasn't even sure it was true. She wasn sure of anything any more.

'Men like your father say they can look into crowd of a thousand kids, and know within second which ones.' Yes, Janice thought. Which ones are worth loving, which ones are like me, worthless. 'Vulnerable needy. You were too big a risk for him because he knew you'd fight him, talk, tell.' What? Janice thought. She' expected him to tell her how valueless she was – too ugly to be loved, too stupid to work out why. 'A strong little girl,' he said. He'd given her something, Janic thought. In the middle of his pain, he'd given her something good to hold on to. She wasn't stupid, wasn' ugly. Just strong. Stronger than Louise. Stronger than Nina. 'Nina envied you, but she was only doing what all big sisters should: taking the rap for you. She still is.'

She heard him start to leave, and turned to look a him for the last time. She couldn't speak to him, didn' dare. But she knew in that moment she'd love him for ever.

Judith and Fitz stood near the doors in the hospital corridor, waiting.

There was nothing else they could do.

Judith wanted to go to Fitz, to be held by him. Cherished. She wanted to tell him she was proud of him for getting the truth out of Janice Cochrane in time for it to make a difference.

She didn't feel she could do any of these things, so instead she stood looking through the glass door at the darkness outside.

She heard a footfall, and turned. A nurse was coming down the corridor towards them. Judith dashed towards the woman, then hesitated, terrified of what she might hear.

The nurse smiled slightly.

'Mark?' Judith said.

'We've made him comfortable,' the nurse said.

Judith stared at her intently, horribly afraid that she might think hospital-speak for something terrible was good news. 'But he's all right?' she persisted.

'He'll be fine,' the nurse said. 'But he needs rest. You should get some too –'

'No, no,' Judith said. 'We're fine.' She glanced at Fitz, to include him in that 'we're'. 'Thank you,' she said. It seemed inadequate. 'Thank you.'

The nurse smiled and left.

Immediately, Fitz took out a cigarette and lit it. He opened the door and the cool night air rushed in.

Judith found that she was smiling. She went over to

Fitz and touched him gently on the hand. He'd done it. He'd saved Mark, just as much as the emergency doctors and nurses.

She should be glad of that. Proud of him. Yet all she could think of was that he'd said he loved his family. How long was it since he'd told her he loved her? Years. And he'd said he'd die for them. For his family. But had he meant her, or just the children? She knew what she thought, but she had to know.

'You say you'd die for your family?' she asked. Fitz wouldn't look at her, just dragged on his cigarette. 'You'd die for your children.' He did look at her now, that level, assessing gaze she'd seen him use on his clients. 'You'd die for your children because they're a part of you.' She wanted him to say something, to stop her saying what came next. He didn't. 'But I don't believe you love me any more than that girl.'

'She's damaged,' Fitz said, as if it were an answer. 'She's confused. She doesn't know what she believes.'

'I meant the other one.'

'So did I.' He sounded surprised.

He was avoiding the issue, and they both knew it. She started to touch him, but she couldn't. She had to know. '*Would* you die for me?' she asked. She did touch him then, lightly with just the tips of her fingers. '*Just* me?'

Answer. Please answer, she thought. But he didn't. Couldn't. Perhaps wouldn't.

And that, in itself, told her everything she needed to know. He moved away, leaving her standing with her hand outstretched from where she'd been touching him.

He went outside. She turned to watch him go, an

w the doors slide shut, as if to seal him off from her
r ever.

She turned and walked away. Away from him, into
e future. Whether they stayed together or not, she was
alking away from him.

As she walked, she slowly picked up speed.

tz stood alone in the cold and the dark. He dragged on
s cigarette, and blue smoke wreathed his face.

He'd been honest with her, that pure honesty that
'd sought all his life. She'd walked away because of
He wasn't sure whether he'd won something.

Or lost everything.

CRACKER

**Cracker novels are available from all
good book shops, but in case of difficulty you can
order them directly from Virgin Publishing.**

Each book costs £4.99. Please add for postage and packing:
   – in the UK / BFPO / Ireland: £1 for the first book and 50p for
each additional book;
   – overseas: £2 for the first book and £1 for each additional book.

You can pay by cheque, made payable to Virgin Publishing Ltd,
or by credit card.

Send your order to:
   Cash Sales Department, Virgin Publishing Ltd,
   332 Ladbroke Grove, London W10 5AH

Please send me the following Cracker novels

Quantit

The Mad Woman In The Attic	by Jim Mortimore	....
To Say I Love You	by Molly Brown	....
One Day A Lemming Will Fly	by Liz Holliday	....
To Be A Somebody	by Gareth Roberts	....
The Big Crunch	by Liz Holliday	....
Men Should Weep	by Jim Mortimore	....
Brotherly Love	by Jim Mortimore	....
Best Boys	by Gareth Roberts	....
True Romance	by Liz Holliday	....

Please tick one box and complete the spaces

☐   I enclose my cheque for £ ....

☐   Please debit my Visa/Access/Mastercard account

        (please delete those not applicable)

        My card number is ....

        and its expiry date is ....

Please send the books to: Name ....

                           Address ....

                           ....

                           ....

                           ....